SUPER

I wasn't prepared for this

Thanks to all the people who helped me edit and con
won't mention you by name, as I feel like there are sti
potentially even spelling errors inside. You shouldn'

this.

To the reader: Please ignore any of those errc

formatting mistakes I probably n

Also, thank you too.

Introduction

I really enjoy drugs. They have always held a special place in my heart. I appreciated smoking a joint or trying out a new high from time to time. However, it had never occurred to me that I could make some money selling the stuff. Then I became one of the most famous drug dealers in the biggest city in America. It happened by accident. I mean, I never intended it to happen that way. It is a long and sordid story. Knowing I had the best marijuana ever concocted on this planet can explain it quickly enough. That does not do the tale justice though. To get an idea of how things can escalate into scary territory, I have to share the details.

I am positive you have heard this story before. It has been told dozens of times in different ways. It gets changed, modified and mystified as it loses what truly happened. I want to set the record straight. You can only hear the true account through me.

Baillargeon

Chapter 1

I loved my life. I also started hating every minute of it. I kept myself busy. I had a job, I had lots of friends and I got laid on a pretty consistent basis by a string of random women. People were jealous of me.

So why did I feel so goddamned depressed?

One of the possible reasons was my brother. I don't remember the last time anybody called him by his actual name. Everyone knew him as 'G'. G was a great guy and I loved him, but supporting him and his exploits was starting to get old. He had been living with me for the past six months.

He said the postman was, "Obviously stealing and destroying my rent cheques." This resulted in his eviction. I had to help him.

I didn't exactly have a lot of room. Not a lot of people in this city do. Especially people with shitty jobs like mine.

I lived in the Lower East Side, always had. When I was younger it was an extremely rough neighbourhood. It was all my mom could afford. Over the past decade we have seen it change. It was turning trendy and was almost a respectable place to live. At least at that price bracket. It was an old neighbourhood and the buildings had been around a long time. Old brick, which stayed some derivative of red but never the same colour, changed from building to building. These bricks were criss-crossed with constant stairs and ladders making up the different fire escapes. People made shoddy patios on the landings. They tried to use the four-square feet of outdoors that were available to them, even if it was illegal and defeated their purpose. They wanted to grow a few plants and potentially sit on their so-called balcony. These balconies covered the entire community, casting shadows that made the place older and scarier. Air conditioning units were the only new addition to many places. They darted out from windows to deal with the inevitable heat summer would bring. A small window unit was usually capable of cooling the tiny apartments averaging five hundred square feet.

My apartment was smaller than average. I did have a bedroom, which I was grateful for. My kitchen, living room, den, dining room and library unfortunately shared a single space. Thank God for the bathroom door.

I was twenty-eight years old and I was sharing a queen sized bed with my little brother. This was enough to make anyone feel down. When G first got there, he was crashing on my couch. When I realized how messy this would make the tiny living room, my small sanctuary from the world, a disaster area, I let him live in the bedroom.

My mom was a fantastic woman, but there was only so much she could do. She did a fine job raising us after our father passed away. When it was only the three of us for so long, she got lonely. It must have been a struggle for her. It made sense for her to leave G to fend for himself.

My dad passed away when I was ten. It was a tough time to lose a father but I had been old enough to learn a few things from him. He was a strong and responsible guy who taught me valuable lessons about hard work, being a man and blazing your own path. Unfortunately, G doesn't remember him.

We didn't have any other family in the city. My dad was an only child and his parents passed away before I had a chance to get to know them. Mom had two sisters somewhere on the West Coast. They haven't talked since the passing of their mother. I didn't get to know any of my aunts, uncles or four cousins I had somewhere out there. My mom tried her best, but it was difficult to do with little money and two young boys who didn't make life any easier. As I grew up I had to look after G most of the time. I understood, but I thought it would stop at some point.

There wasn't much for us to do as children, so we sometimes got in trouble. Our mom tried to keep us busy and we tried a few sports. I was never good at any of them and it wasn't the most affordable thing to do. I wasn't too bad at tennis, but I was awful at golf. The one thing my mom spoiled us with was racing. She said my dad used to do it as a young man in his twenties. We got into the odd race track tournament on go karts. I loved it. However, there weren't a lot of places to do that in the city anymore.

As my mom spent most of her life struggling to make ends meet, she finally met a nice man. When the relationship got serious she had to take a serious step. He was some oilfield guy from Canada who used to do a lot of finance business here when they met. When he took a new job in their head office in Calgary, my mom took the second leap of her life. It came fast, but when you hit a certain age you apparently don't waste any time. I was twenty four at the time and after four years of dating, I was capable of coming to terms with this but my brother never did. He was still too young and had not gotten his feet underneath himself yet. When my mom decided to move, G was stuck in limbo. He was old enough to move out on his own, but he was young enough to consider going with my mom. He had no desire to move to Canada. He was on his own in the big city at eighteen.

At least the guy she married had some serious money. Not that he shared any with my brother and me. We hardly knew the man. He was cordial with us, but that was for mom's sake. He did fly us to Calgary once a year for Canadian Thanksgiving. Their Thanksgiving is in October for some odd reason. It was the one time of year we could get together.

That was the extent of my world travels. To a place known as Cow Town to celebrate a holiday Canadians celebrated during the wrong month. We had got back three weeks prior, and the visit went well. We saw some funny shit in Canada. For a country so similar to ours, they are so different.

So with my mother out of town it was up to me to make sure G did not end up dead in an alley somewhere. That was my main goal. Then I wanted him in his own place. Since he would need money, he was going to need a job. I woke him up every morning when I headed to work in the hopes he might get up and do something. This morning was no different.

"G, I gotta get moving. Get your ass out of bed."

"Mghhhh," was all I got in reply.

I went into the bathroom to freshen up before leaving. I looked in the mirror. Sometimes I forgot what a disgusting sight I was. I was growing a mustache for this charity called Movember to raise money for prostate cancer research. Men would grow push brooms on their lip for November to boost awareness. It was not hard to notice the guys with mustaches who shouldn't have mustaches. That would bring up discussions about prostate cancer and open the opportunity to raise funds. It was not exactly popular in the city, with a big campaign here like other places, so it was embarrassing. G had learned about it on our trip to Canada. They raise a lot of money for charity there. He thought it was hilarious and had convinced several people to participate, including most of the guys at my work. I would have never heard the end of it if I hadn't joined. So there I was with a thick dark cookie duster and curly black hair. I wasn't sure if I was fortunate or not that my soup strainer came in so thick and quick. As I observed myself in the mirror I gave the obligatory check out. I was still quite fit, and even with the facial fur, I thought handsome. My mom told me I would be. I quickly brushed my teeth, threw on my uniform for work and was ready to head out.

I kicked the bed hard as I walked by. I wanted to make certain G wasn't trying to fall back asleep.

"I'm up, I'm up," grumbled the pile of meat under the blankets.

"Use this morning to get up and look for a job. I want to see some progress when I get home from work tonight. And clean up your fucking mess in the kitchen while you're at it."

"Ya ya ya ya."

If I didn't have to work I could have stayed on top of him. Maybe he would have got his shit done. Unfortunately, without a supervisor I didn't expect much from him. What were the chances he could have landed a job with that greasy mustache anyway? He should not have been allowed near playgrounds or schools, let alone land a job.

Somebody had to pay the bills though. It was time for me to head to work.

Chapter 2

My job was shitty, and I mean in a literal sense. When I was younger my mom convinced me that working with my hands was one of my best options. It never sat well with me that she thought I was slow. To be fair, I didn't exactly bring home the most impressive report cards. She would have got tired of hearing, "He means well, but..." at the parent/teacher conferences. Looking back, I deserved the shit I took from the teachers as I was not making their jobs easy. They took it the wrong way though. They thought I acted out because I was slow and didn't get the material. Actually, I was bored. I understood it and found the work simple enough to not give it much thought. I held this fact back as I didn't want to come off as a nerd. Cool kids don't try.

So my mom convinced herself I should get into a trade. It wasn't the best reasoning for me to pursue it, but in the end it wasn't a terrible decision. People in this city don't exactly know how to work with their hands. Even during the terrible economy, plumbing had problems, and we were there to fix it. I made decent money and could keep myself busy. My boss was a big fan of mine. He always had work for me to keep me coming in every day.

I got to work this particular Monday morning and I knew my day was off to a terrible start. Dubs ended up arriving at the same time and walked in with me. He had a big shit eating grin behind his disgusting, thin and crooked mustache as he stared at me. I think he knew I didn't like him and he relished in it. Either that, or he was clueless and he actually liked me. I don't know what it was about him I disliked so much. I just hated his face. I can't explain it any better than that. This was kind of weird because people told us we looked alike. Sometimes they thought we were brothers. He was at least forty pounds heavier and almost a foot shorter, so those comments felt like insults.

Our names even sounded similar. When he started working at our shop people kept getting us confused on work orders. For ease sake, he opted to take a nick name. His name began with a W, so he took the liberty of nick naming himself Dubs. No wonder I fucking hated this guy. Who gives themselves a nick name?

"Morning," he offered in my direction with that fucking smile of his.

Forced into a response I mumbled, "Morning," back. Just because I didn't like him didn't mean I could be an asshole. My mother would have scolded me for that kind of behavior. She would tell me there is nothing to gain in being cruel. Therefore, I continued to be as kind as I could muster.

We walked into the office and got our morning assignments. I grabbed one of the company vans and headed out.

I did three jobs that morning. One was doing some installs at an expanding restaurant. The next was repairing some lines at another restaurant. I don't know if it's the number of restaurants in this city, or the type of people running them that causes them to have so many plumbing issues. Either way, I spent most of my time in them. The majority of my visits, after being in their kitchen, I knew I would never return as a paying customer. I also lost trust in the food safety board for the A banners in the windows. The things I witnessed in supposedly clean restaurants would make a rat gag. Which, they probably did. They were in the restaurants to see what I saw too.

My third job before lunch was to a private residence in a nice part of town. I knocked and it took quite a while before a slow moving senior answered the door.

This lady was old. I mean, I feared for her safety while she was alone in the house, old. Sometimes the job could be depressing with the type of places you went and the people you met. The majority of work was usually conducted at businesses. Employees and owners don't have time to tinker away and fix things themselves. They have a business to run. Every once in a while you got calls like these. This old lady made me feel so damn depressed. Don't get me wrong, she was the sweetest old woman I have ever met. When I arrived, she greeted me at the door with such hospitality. There were literally milk and cookies out. I never knew either of my grandmas, but I could see myself adopting this one as my own.

Her house was beautiful and she evidently had plenty of money. The issue I was struggling with was the job was too simple. A tiny clogged drain was a five minute fix for me. I almost puked while doing it though. Pulling old, grey, long, fermented hairs in a ball out of a sink was like discovering a lab rat in there. For being a plumber, my gag reflex was pretty high in these situations. I had to turn my head and hold back vomit as I regained my composure more than once.

There was another reason a simple job like this depressed me. Someone she knew should have been able to handle it. A friend, a neighbor, a child, a grandchild. This lady obviously didn't have one of those to help her with these simple things. There were pictures of her husband around the house, but none of children. If I were to guess, they were quite the power couple in their heyday and decided they were better off without children. With the husband seemingly passed on, she was lonely. I wondered if she regretted her 'no children' decision. Since she aged, she probably had few people in her life. She has likely watched her friends slip away and has nobody younger than her around. I struggled to imagine what kind of life that would be.

She was anxious to have company in the house. She asked me questions the entire time, mostly wondering if I had a wife and children at home. I informed her I was living the bachelor life.

"A young, handsome man such as yourself? You seem like a nice boy. You will meet a lovely woman soon," was her reply. Old ladies loved me for some reason. I took solace in the fact that if I didn't find someone in thirty years, I could finally settle down with one.

As the job was short, there was not much time for talking and I could see her disappointment when I had to leave. I wouldn't have put it past this lady to sabotage parts of her house to have a recurring visit from repairmen like me to talk to. She would surely suffer disenchantment from this idea, as a lot of them are not as polite as I attempt to be.

As I left, it made my recent depression run deeper. The last thing I wanted to do is end up like that old lady. Not that it was that bad, I only wanted something different for myself. A wife. Some children. A family. When I was in situations like this it was tough not to reminisce. I would think about past relationships and why they didn't work.

As I was driving to my next job, I thought of the twenty-six year old virgin I couldn't commit to, I was scared to take the next step with her as she may have become too attached. I was confident it wasn't going to go anywhere. If you meet a twenty-six year old virgin, assume they might be boring. Who wants to spend their Saturday nights going for cheesecake and coffee and settling on the couch for cuddles for the evening? She couldn't spend the nights because she had to go to church in the morning. At first, this was what I thought I needed. Someone to settle me down and take me in a new direction. In the end, it wasn't the lack of sex that ended it. The root cause of the breakup was cake, coffee, cuddles and Christ. It got boring fast.

There were many other women that didn't work for all sorts of reasons. It may sound terrible, but as you get older, bitches get crazier. There are reasons why they are still single. I tried to date, but I almost never passed the third outing. There would always be some quality I wouldn't want in a wife or a mother, and I would cut it short right there. I didn't want to be wasting my time or theirs. Also, I was fearful I would be dating some bimbo I didn't like when an amazing girl would come along. I wouldn't want to be that sleaze ball cheating on his girlfriends.

My last true girlfriend and I stayed together for almost three years. This was over five years ago now. Her name was Pauline and I should have known better. She was the life of the party. She had a magnetic personality that people were really drawn to. She had a large group of friends and her social calendar was never empty. People liked hanging out with her.

I think I may have been in love, so much so I didn't notice how little she was in love with me. Don't get me wrong, we were awesome together, but I knew her heart was never into it. I was cautious not to get too close or be too 'boyfriend' for her liking. I worried I might scare her off. Older me wants to go back and kick younger me's ass for not figuring that shit out sooner.

The problem was Pauline was too much fun. We had a blast together. When I was with her I thought she was everything I was looking for. When we weren't together, I thought she was the worst person in the world. She neglected my existence and never considered my feelings if we were not located in the same room. I would spend a week not seeing her and would want to break up with her the entire time. When she came back and we hung out, I forgot about it. I called her my weekday girlfriend. During the week she wanted to hang out, go on dates and do fun activities together. Come the weekend she was about big plans and adventures, but she neglected to include me in most of them. It's amazing how looking back, it is easy to see how bad the situation was. Your friends will tell you they were thinking it the entire time.

I broke it off when Pauline was getting too close to one of her guy 'friends'. I accused her of cheating and the relationship blew up. She still denies it, yet she ended up marrying this so called 'friend' a few years later. If she wasn't banging him, she was thinking about it. That constitutes cheating for me. The consolation of being right never made me feel better about the situation.

When I eventually told her we couldn't see each other anymore, the conversation got ugly. I was doing the breaking, but it was because she wasn't into it and I needed to move on. I wanted an explanation for why she wasn't into me after two years of dating. The things that bothered her would have probably been better left unsaid. She hated that I was a plumber and she was afraid we would have a boring life. I was not pleased by the conversation. I may have mentioned some words along the lines of, "You will regret this."

I wasn't threatening her with violence or anything. I just thought one day she would regret not locking me down. I was destined for a better life than what I was currently doing. Unfortunately, you judge yourself by the potential you believe you are capable of. Everyone else judges you by the actions you actually accomplish. I hadn't accomplished shit.

Not that my threats of regret were motivating or depressing me those days. I did feel shitty about what I could have been doing though. I wanted to start my own business. I wanted to travel the world. I wanted to be great.

Chapter 3

The weekend was upon us after a long five days of work. It was late Friday afternoon when everyone was back at the office, returning equipment and cleaning up from the week's activities. A colleague of mine, Steve, was having a particularly rough week. His wife had left him the week before and he was struggling to keep it together. I had picked up two jobs for him already and was helping him clean his van out after his last job.

"How about I take you for a beer Steve? Let's grab some eats and some drinks. It's on me." I was trying anything to alleviate the poor guy's pain. He was a sad sack of a man. He was an excellent father, but his wife never respected him. I remember the first time I met her. I felt bad for him. I knew he would be a doormat. His wife had apparently been sleeping around with multiple men. One day, she decided to run off with one of them. Steve didn't deserve this. Neither did his kids.

"Thanks a lot man, but Rebecca is dropping the kids off for the weekend so she can head out of town on some holiday with Paul." He changed his voice and inflection on the word Paul and filled it with hate and disgust. "I do appreciate the offer, and maybe next week, as it will be a tough weekend. This isn't the easiest thing to explain to the girls," he finished. He grabbed his bag and made his way out the door.

Dubs made his way over to me in the meantime.

"I'll go for a drink with ya," he offered.

"Sorry Dubs, I got plans."

I turned and walked away.

It was a weekend to let off some steam. I got home and G had a case of cold beer waiting for me. He cracked two when I walked in the door. Sometimes G knew how to treat a brother. It may have been purchased with spare change found around the apartment, but it was thoughtful nonetheless. We drank a few beers while talking about what we could get up to that evening, running through our list of friends that might be up to something. He asked me to give Dubs a call. They got along for some reason. There was no way I was about to invite him out though, and G knew that. He grinned at me when he knew he was pushing my buttons. We were trying to call up some girls to go out with, but none were around or wanted to hang out. It was going to be just the bros. As if sharing a bed with him wasn't enough.

We went to one of our usual places, a pub where G and I played our usual games with women at the bar. G was quite taller than me, but not close to my weight. He was boney jagged corners. All joints. That didn't mean he couldn't do well with the ladies. What he lacked in physical prowess he made up for in wit and attitude. Something about an unemployed free spirit many women found attractive. I could never figure it out. He even asked girls what they thought of his current mustache. He didn't lack confidence. Unfortunately for him, he was skilled at opening doors but had trouble closing the deal. That's where I came in. He could establish relationships with women, the art of the cold call, and I got to walk up and start chatting after. Sometimes smoothing over some idiot remark by the pointy bastard. It didn't hurt that I was much older than him. Women love the older and more mature option.

We had a lot of fun doing this. We enjoyed meeting people. We tried to see what kind of stupid things we could get away with saying or doing. Sometimes this led us into awkward or strange situations making for funny stories. There were crazy parties, crazy women, and crazy mind bending hallucinogens. We had fun. It was a change having my brother around. I used to get into a lot of trouble. It wasn't uncommon for my night to end rehashing fight stories for G when I got home. He looked up to me, and when he was of age, I was finally well past this stage. I didn't want him to fall in the same trap I did. I stuck to teaching him everything I knew about picking up women.

On this particular weekend we headed to the bars on both Friday and Saturday, meeting up with random groups of friends. We met a lot of girls. It was an enjoyable time and I got three different phone numbers. The one I got on Friday night received a text from me when I was drunk the following night. I guess I was kind of hoping to get a random hookup out of it. It didn't take. She was classier than I had taken her for. Not interested in a drunken hookup and after that text she wasn't interested in me in general. She stopped answering my texts and I knew it could never progress. I felt dejected and lost interest in the other two. I didn't bother messaging them.

Saturday night I ditched early to get home before G. My recent unhappiness and the rejection from that girl had me feeling down in the dumps. I needed to burn one. I decided to walk home as I had the forethought of bringing a joint with me. I stopped at the park a few blocks from my house and lit up. I must have laid in the park for twenty-minutes staring into the sky. Not the safest thing to do at that hour, so I got myself up and walked home. I got back shortly after one and fell asleep on the couch watching late night cartoons. I didn't hear G walk in.

Sunday I had my regular hangover routine. I made some breakfast for G while we initiated recovery from the consecutive night bender. I spent a bit of time on the phone with my mother, catching her up on the week of activities. We chatted every Sunday, but our phone calls were superficial. I didn't quite fill her in on the gritty details of what we did, or how low G was sinking. She wanted to know how he was doing or if he was working yet. She put a lot of pressure on me to be responsible for him. She had to question some of my past bad habits, as if they could still be poisoning him. Aside from that, she had her regular questions and statements. She wanted to know if I was seeing anyone, afraid I would never settle down. This always led to her questioning my drinking habits and then scolding me that my liver would never last. Every once in a while she would compliment me, but it consistently felt backhanded. She would tell me how smart I was and how clever I could be, but that would make her question why I wasn't accomplishing more. Thanks Mom.

That afternoon I had my visit with my little brother. Not G. I was a volunteer at Big Brothers Big Sisters of America. I had joined a couple years earlier. I would like to say it was for the children, but when I joined I thought it would be a way to meet women. Don't get me wrong, I'm glad to be helping out kids, but there also happened to be a lot of social events where I met a wide variety of nice women. It's where I had met the virgin.

As I got further involved though, my priorities did change. Lots of these kids needed a positive male role model. As I grew up without my dad through my formative years, I could see a lot of myself in many of the poor buggers I worked with. Some of them were cool little bastards too. I was sticking this program out way longer than I thought I would. I actually enjoyed it. Lots of these guys looked up to me, and it made me want to be a better person. It taught me a lot about kids. I think it not only prepared me for having my own children, but made me anxious to find the lady I could finally do that with.

This was a pretty typical weekend though, and going back to work on Monday was a drag. My slow decline into depression was worsening due to my nocturnal exploits. I never verbalized it, but my lifestyle was eating away at me. I wasn't happy with what I was becoming. It's not like my work was causing any of it. With so much time driving and the mindless activities I had to perform, I had too much time to think about my personal life. I sometimes wondered what it would be like to be too busy at work to think about stuff. Maybe time would fly by. I often wondered if I should have gone to college, or maybe settled for the mind numbing repetitiveness of a fast food restaurant. It was too late to switch careers by then either way.

It didn't help when I got in Monday morning to learn Steve had quit, effective immediately. Apparently his wife had no intention of coming back from her holiday with her new man, 'Paul'. Steve was going to take his girls and move back out to the Midwest. I knew it was the right decision for the kids. However, my heart still broke for the guy. It was tough to see a family you know disintegrate in front of you. Steve was a good dad though and I was confident he could get his kids through the tough times.

I did a few standard jobs that day, but late in the afternoon I had a call to a residence. As these calls were a roll of the dice on whether or not they would be interesting, difficult, uncomfortable or crazy, I was looking forward to the randomness of it. Today I would be installing a garburator. This was usually easy work if someone had not mangled the plumbing or cupboards under the sink.

I walked up to an apartment building and rang the buzzer.

"Who is it?" asked the voice from a tiny black speaker in the wall.

It was a woman. Sounded like a good looking young one too. That was a shame. In my experience, that meant there was a high probability she was unattractive and possibly overweight. The type perfect for radio. I introduced myself and the door buzzed open. I made my way up the few flights of stairs to the apartment.

I knocked on the door. I stood there, curious. I wanted to prove my inappropriate thoughts correct, thus making them justified. It opened, revealing the most beautiful creature I have ever seen. Apparently super models require plumbing too. I thought they found random dudes to do things like this, but for free. This was a first. I opened my mouth to speak but my brain did not keep up with the situation. It was stuck focusing on the anomaly before me. I stammered when I went to speak.

"Ga ga good afternoon ma'am." Ma'am. When the fuck had I ever said ma'am? I was going to have to pull my shit together.

"Hi there. Please, come in. And please, no ma'am stuff. Call me Aida. Can I get you anything to drink while you work?"

"No thanks. I should be fine."

She led me into the apartment and showed me the small kitchen. The place had a similar layout and size to mine but it was different. There was art and pictures on the walls, the colors of the furniture matched and the air smelled of wildflowers. I lived in an apartment. This girl lived in her home.

She went over to the cupboards and I found it odd she kept some cups in the bottom drawer near her sink. However weird I found it, it was my new favourite drawer when she bent down to grab one. She was a tall girl, with a beautiful body and a tiny waist. At that moment I thanked God for Lululemon (later I found out the man I should have thanked was Chip Wilson). She grabbed two glasses and filled them with water. I guess I was drinking water.

My next thought was pure panic. I remembered I had a stupid fucking mustache on my face. I became self-conscious about my appearance. She turned around to face me with a glass of water in hand, placed it on the counter and told me it was there if I needed it. I was too busy holding my hand over my mouth to respond. I was desperately trying to disguise the fact that I currently had a sexual predator's appearance.

"So, before you get started, I have a weird question," she began.

I was deathly afraid of what was about to happen next. My heart raced as this girl could have went anywhere with that opening statement. I didn't know if I was I was capable of hearing it.

"Is that mustache for real? Or please tell me you know what Movember is."

I burst out laughing. Wow, was I relieved. She was a big fan of Movember. An old family friend got prostate cancer a few years ago, so she had some involvement in fundraising before. She also got a kick out of the mustaches she would see throughout the month. We chatted about it as I prepped.

I got down and took a look under the sink. She took a seat at the table a few feet away with a clear view of me working. She sat there, legs crossed and her body poised. Sitting politely one could say. She kept chatting while I worked. She surprised me when she told me she wasn't a super model, but a librarian. It was hard to picture her as a book worm. She was equally impressed when we discussed books and how much I knew. I had taken up reading about a year ago and had read a bunch of classics. My timing couldn't have been better.

We got to talk about Hemmingway, Steinbeck and Orwell. I got excited at the prospect that some of our favorite books lined up. We talked about 1984 in detail (the book, not the year). I was glad I got to show off my intellectual side. Even if I had my head under her sink and my hands covered in grimy grease.

We talked about her job and how much she liked it, though it paid absolute shit. I knew little about working at a library these days, as I thought books were no longer used by our current generation. I got mine through Amazon. If I had known librarians looked like this, I would have owned a library card.

I was curious about a librarian's career so I asked a lot of questions. She talked while I shouted out a question from time to time. Turns out she spent her time building literacy programs for families and kids, trying to get them interested in reading. It seemed like a noble thing to do. It impressed me. She was one of those lucky people who gets satisfaction from their work.

"How do you like your job?" she asked me, as if reading my mind.

"It pays the bills," I replied, looking at her while taking a drink of water. I could tell by her look that my answer did not sufficiently answer her question. She seemed disappointed by my response. I would have to go deeper, regardless of how little I enjoyed talking about my work and career choices.

"I mean, it's alright. I like working with my hands and it's nice to finish projects and be useful to people. I just wish I owned my own business or at least did something more meaningful than fixing clogged drains. Like, maybe I should have gone to school. Wear a suit like those people walking outside," I told her in earnest.

"What's wrong with being a plumber? My dad was an electrician, and I have respect for tradesmen. Plus, you have a real sweet uniform. Somebody was clever that day." She smiled slyly. I couldn't tell if she was being playful or mocking me. I chose to believe she was being playful.

"Ya. My boss likes to think so. Anyway, I am finished up here. Thanks for being so friendly through this process. Made it real easy. I don't deal with a lot of young people. They tend to let plumbing problems get worse out of laziness or they aren't willing to spend any money." I explained to her. Our interaction did make my day.

"Well it was a fun visit. I was expecting an old fat man. I picked your company because of your slogan. I didn't want to see that fat old man's ass crack. Although it was weird letting in a rapist," she referred to my mustache. "If you had aviator sunglasses on I don't think I would have opened the door."

"Well I'm glad I was able to help, and that you could see past my mustache. I swear there is a handsome man behind this somewhere," I said as I waved my hand over my face.

"I believe it," she said, looking right at me.

I hesitated, but I was confident that was the invitation I needed. She was definitely into me. Then again, maybe she was just being nice. She was a smoke show and I had my head underneath her sink for forty-five minutes. This was the moment that was an issue. Convincing myself to take a shot at it. Luckily I had built up a strong defense to rejection, so I thought I could handle it. I began to stammer through an awkward moment.

"Well thanks again, I really enjoyed your company. Maybe, sometime later this week, I could perhaps take you out for a drink, wearing some regular clothes and not having my hands dirty. You know, if you are interested."

"Are you asking me on a date?" she asked coyly.

"I guess so. Sorry if this is inappropriate. I shouldn't be bothering you. This is not what you paid for in our service. I'm so sorry." I turned to leave with my tail between my legs. I wondered if this would get back to my office. I was so embarrassed. Trying this while on the job left me feeling sheepish. I would have looked completely dejected and stupid.

"I am just messing with you," she said with a big smile, "I would like that. Are you still going to have that mustache?" she asked. My emotions did a full one hundred eighty degree swing as I turned around with a giant smile on my face.

"Sadly yes. I have to keep it for another two weeks until December, and I would prefer to not have to wait until then to take you out. Hopefully that's not an issue?"

"No, that's alright. It looks great on you," she said with a hint of sarcasm. "You got my info on your invoice there. It will make you creepier when you have to steal my number from there. I'll hear from you?"

"For sure. I'll call you later in the week to go on a date this weekend."

"Are you going to call like a man, or are you going to text me like a teenager?" she asked.

"Well I guess you answered that question for me. Expect to hear my voice later this week."

"Super."

I turned and gave a soft bye with a wave as the door was closing behind me. She had already put that phone number on the invoice before I had asked her for it, so I was confident I didn't get a fake number. It turned out to be a delightful day.

Baillargeon

Chapter 4

I had not been that nervous in a long time. I couldn't remember the last time I called a girl for a date. Not since texting became a thing. If she hadn't asked for the phone call, I would have texted for sure.

I didn't remember how to do it. My heart was racing when I went to dial the number. Before I pressed the dial button I put the phone down. What happened if she didn't answer? Do I leave a message? If so, what does it say? If I didn't leave a message, I would have to call back. How many times can I do that with those missed calls from a strange number?

Worse yet, what happens if she does answer? Do I make small talk or jump straight into asking about a date? I wasn't ready. I couldn't believe it was happening to me. I thought my confidence was stronger than that.

I actually sat down and made notes. A script for a message if she didn't answer. Discussion points I could bring up to make small talk if necessary. Three different plans for dates in case she didn't like the first two. It was a loose map of fluid possibilities. The plan was nothing, planning was everything.

With that panic attack out of the way, I was somewhat prepared. I was able to pick up my phone again.

When it rang I felt my stomach fill with uncertainty. My heart rate picked up and I became nervous once more. I understood why people used to hang up mid ring. With call display, that was no longer an option. I was doing this.

Thank God she answered. I didn't want to have to use my voicemail script. It wasn't good. It would have sounded forced. Probably because it would have been.

The phone call went better than expected. Not as difficult as I had psyched myself up for. Once I introduced myself and had a few pleasantries out of the way, I asked her to go for some drinks on Friday night. She was so easy going. She obliged and I picked a location she agreed with. It was quick and simple, which was perfect. I was able to keep some material for our date.

-      -   -   -   -   -   -

I met her at a pub. If she looked good in her comfort clothes at her house, she was gorgeous when she went out. She had long blonde hair. It wasn't straight, but it wasn't curly. It just kind of bounced down off her shoulders. It framed her face in the most magnificent way. I immediately got drawn in to her big blue eyes. She was beautiful, and didn't need to show off to prove it. She dressed in a conservative manner compared to girls these days, but it still emphasized her athletic figure. She was a peach.

I stood up to greet her. Luckily, I was also dressed semi-casually. I went back and forth for an hour in front of the mirror on whether to wear a jacket and slacks or jeans and a polo. Considering the venue, I hoped it would be casual. Thankfully, our styles matched. Crisis one was averted. Now it was up to my brain and mouth to avoid the embarrassing stuff.

We ordered a couple drinks to start. One time I had ordered a cocktail on a first date and my date ordered a beer. I felt emasculated and decided never to let that happen again. Now I went with my standard beer. She got a beer too and we chatted. We talked for hours. About anything and everything. We talked so much and got through the boring first date stuff so fast we were talking about serious issues. We talked of our bad habits, like how much we liked to drink and smoke. Turns out she liked to blaze too. One of those types who swears if people smoked grass, it would solve the world's problems.

We hit all the topics, including the ones they tell you never to mention with new people. Politics, race, abortions and religion. We tackled them. She told me about the dating world as a girl, and the douchebags she had to deal with. She managed to get me talking of my childhood. A few beers, a location change and a bottle of wine had my tongue loose. Maybe exceeding where it should have been.

"Well, I was kind of an angry child. My dad passed away when I was ten. Without him around I maybe got into shit. I had what some may call a short fuse. I tended to instigate a fight now and then. I have beaten some guys up which I don't feel great about. I have taken beatings a few times which I feel even worse about."

I could tell she was interested in this topic. Maybe because she was into the dirty side of things, or maybe because she was interested to hear how I grew up. I had trouble telling the difference because I had never talked to anyone about this stuff before. Wading into unfamiliar territory, I continued.

"It's weird how it can snowball from there. It starts to become a part of who you are. My brother and I used to egg people on, trying to start fights. We gave ourselves a nickname, but I am too embarrassed to repeat it. It was stupid. My brother idolized me and I was leading us down a stupid path. Next thing you know you are twenty-one years old and getting in fights at bars. At that age and surrounded by those types of people, they are no longer impressed. When I was twenty-four some guy was pissing me off. He was quite a bit bigger than me and thought he was tough. I guess he thought I would back down or turn and run when he threatened me. When I didn't, he got mad and threw a punch. It happened fast, but he was on the ground bleeding and I was standing over him. Two of his buddies came at me and I took a few hits but landed damaging blows back in their direction. I had got on top of one guy and was about to pummel him when someone grabbed me from behind. I turned around, fist cocked, and the poor guy's girlfriend was screaming and crying. I stood up and she knelt down to hold him. She stared up at me, tears running down her face. The mortified look said volumes. I scanned the room and I had not impressed anyone. They were scared of me. It made me sick. Usually after a fight the adrenaline was pumping and it would be the most incredible high. This was the first time I felt ashamed. I could have walked away before it came to that, but I didn't. Instead, the usual response came over me and it sort of happened. I didn't have control over the situation, and maybe the crowd saw that. I certainly felt it. I haven't thrown a punch since."

I sat there in silence for a minute. I got nervous that I blew it.

"I shouldn't have said anything. You think I am a psycho, don't you?"

"Not in the least. You learned from it, didn't you? It's good you no longer do that, but weren't a ton of girls impressed by that kind of stuff?"

"Not the type I was looking for I guess," I responded.

"Right answer," she said back.

It was slow going getting the conversation back up and running after that serious topic. Soon enough we were laughing and had moved on to better things. She was amazing.

By the end of the date, we had spent approximately eight hours together. Quite a few drinks were shared. I was feeling quite drunk, which I believed would make her flat out drunk. I was confident my weight and slight history of alcoholism meant I could handle my booze better. It was time to call it a night. I didn't want her to take a cab home by herself so I asked if I could escort her there. My place was past it anyway. I also had a giant crush on her and did not want to leave her.

We arrived in front of her place and I asked the cabbie to wait a minute. He looked hesitant, but decided he would trust me that I would come back. I suppose the mustache doesn't remove my credibility like I thought.

I walked Aida up to her front door. We stood there as I told her how much fun I had and how I hoped we got to do it again real soon. She agreed. I finally leaned in to do what I was waiting to do the whole night at the bar and restaurant. I gave her a kiss goodnight.

Over the next couple weeks we spent almost every day together. We went for drinks, dinners, and movies. I even introduced her to my brother. It was the happiest two weeks of my life to that point. We got to learn so much about each other, it brought us closer. Aida was the most special person I had ever met. I would say she was almost a hippy, without the real annoying hippy qualities like not shaving or bathing. She had an appreciation for people, the earth and healthy foods. We shared in the fact that we both liked to smoke grass, and we indulged a couple times together. While high, we had conversations that took on a life of their own. They seemed to snowball into deep territory I had never ventured with anyone before. They eventually caused me to re-evaluate my life and make me want to be a better man. I was so enamoured with how proud she was of her work. How fulfilling she found it. She loved to hear of my good deeds with the Big Brother program and encouraged me to believe I was worthy of being a role model for kids. I withheld my reasons for joining, but she didn't need to know and I appreciated her thinking that much of me.

We were keeping ourselves busy almost every night on dates. The problem was what that meant for my bank account. I think Aida recognized this. It was growing customary for her to attempt to split bills when we went out. I argued with her every time. She countered, saying I couldn't afford to spoil her. She happened to be right, but when I first let it happen it felt like I was inefficient as a man.

It was now the end of November and my brother and I had raised eight hundred dollars for prostate research with our mustaches. I had told Aida I was thinking of keeping my Selleck Stache so she offered to donate one hundred on the last day if I shaved it off. Once I finally did she said she could no longer see me anymore. It turns out the mustache was what made me attractive. She thought she was so fucking funny.

I was glad the experiment was over. I was tired of that fucking stache. G was already recruiting for next year. I vowed I would not be involved. I hoped I would have more important things on the go.

Chapter 5

I knew right from the beginning. I was so nervous to acknowledge it. It was only a few weeks into dating when I was confident in dropping the L-bomb, but I held out for months. I could tell it was on the tip of her tongue as well and I thought I could wait her out. I didn't want to be the first to say it.

The day before Valentine's Day I was at a friend's house visiting him and his wife. They loved Aida, but she wasn't with me at the time. One of the few times they saw me without her since we met. His wife asked if I had told her how I felt. When I said I hadn't, his wife stared me right in the eye and said, "Don't be a pussy."

It struck me hard as she wasn't one to use that kind of language. She knew me well and knew I couldn't ignore it. She really liked Aida, more than any other girl I had brought around. She was just happy to see me with someone other than Pauline. She wanted to see me with Aida and she was pressuring me as though I needed to hear it to do something.

On Valentine's the following day, Aida and I both agreed to have somewhat of an anti-Valentine's Day. We picked up a case of beer, a bottle of wine and a bucket of Kentucky Fried Chicken. We camped out in her living room, got drunk and watched TV. She was my kind of girl. Even full of KFC, we had sex. It was the romantic day of the year after all. We were lying in bed next to each other and I wanted to say the word. It was right there, I couldn't hold it any longer though. My friend had pushed me over the edge.

"You know I love you right?" What a fucking way to say it. I was a Casanova.

She laughed at me.

"Oh ya?" was her response.

"Come on now, don't make me feel more uncomfortable than I already am. This isn't something I'm used to."

She teased me for several agonizing minutes. I knew she had the same feelings for me, but she was going to make me squirm first. I possibly should have played it more smoothly.

Finally she stopped, got serious and asked, "Do you want to try again stud?"

I gave her a full passionate kiss, pulled away, stared straight into her eyes and said "I love you. I am so happy we met and I am lucky to have you."

"I love you too," she replied softly. A weight lifted off my shoulders when she said it back. This was followed by a wave of pure happiness. I was lying next to this amazing woman who uttered those words. I knew I would never want to let her go.

I was conflicted trying to understand how I had gotten so lucky. Honestly, she was out of my league. I am a confident individual and I think highly of myself. Still, I believed this girl could get anyone she wanted and she was with me. It made me uncomfortable.

One night she brought up the game where you list three celebrities you are allowed to sleep with if given the opportunity. Doing so would not constitute as cheating. I refused to play. I told her it wasn't a fair game because I believed she could pull it off. I didn't think I stood a chance with Jessica Alba, Natalie Portman, or Helen Mirren. Therefore, I didn't want to play. She called me a poor sport. I think I dodged a bullet. I would not have been comfortable with her sleeping with Justin Timberlake.

Over the next four months things got even better. I was over the moon to have found someone who I connected with that well. Everything worked for us and we were both fully committed right from the start. No games.

There was only one other issue in our relationship aside from my own insecurities. I was forced into a situation I didn't like and I knew there was nothing I could do about it. It started during a standard week. The best thing to note was Dubs was on holidays, so I didn't have to deal with him at work. Aida was worked up because her best friend Daisy had called and said she met someone and she was in love. She asked Aida if she and I would come out for a double date to meet her new beau.

"Daisy is so excited to introduce me to this new guy of hers. She hasn't told me anything about him yet, but she is really excited about this. She met him a week ago and they have spent every night together since, which is why I haven't talked to her. She insisted I bring you along so we can all go out for drinks," Aida explained while we made our way to the restaurant.

Aida and I arrived early. Daisy and her mystery man were nowhere to be seen. We grabbed a table and a couple of drinks to start. When they arrived, my heart sank. There was Daisy and her new man. Daisy introduced him to Aida, then turned to me and said, "I believe you two know each other?"

Aida reached under the table and put a hand on my thigh. She knew how I felt about this guy. She heard about him several times when I came home from work. She was talking to me through this gesture. She was telling me 'I know, I know, but play nice.'

"Hey Dubs. How's it going? How has your week of holidays been?" I squeaked out through the shock.

Apparently they met randomly at some coffee shop. They had talked and got around to making the connection that they both knew me. This assisted the relationship along. They thought it may be uncomfortable for us, so Daisy said they would keep it a secret. She would hate that she would come between friends. What had Dubs been telling this poor woman?

Though everything else was going well, I was now forced into hanging out with Dubs outside of work from time to time. After getting to know him better, I disliked him further. Turns out he wasn't aware of my contempt for him, but was that naive. I usually pride myself in finding the best in people and getting along with them on some level. I could not find it with Dubs. He was bipolar in how nice he could be, yet also the most disgusting and crass individual ever. I hated listening to his constant stories about nothing. He would continually laugh maniacally at his own jokes. It was painful. When he didn't like something, he threw out an evil and childish sound. It was a sound along the lines of 'nghhhhaaaaa!' It was so juvenile, stupid and it should have been embarrassing for him. It embarrassed me. He thought it was cool.

I don't know how Daisy stomached it.

Dubs was a small complaint though. Other than the odd double date and seeing him every work day, I still had some of my time free of him. If I wasn't so happy with Aida I may have snapped.

I would handle the worst kind of people out there if I had to. I was in love with the girl. In the six months following the day we met, we hung out all the time and I continued to live the life I had dreamed of. I began staying at her place most of the time. In the meantime, my brother slowly took over my apartment even though I was paying for it. It forced me to crash with her as my place was being transformed. Apparently my presence was what kept my brother maintaining a certain level of cleanliness. Aida didn't mind having me, and I was happy to spend my nights with her.

For our sixth month anniversary of our first date, a day she remembered and reminded me of, I wanted to go above and beyond. I told her I wanted to take her on a trip. At dinner we discussed the possibilities of Mexico, Hawaii, and Thailand. She was ecstatic to talk about it. Her eyes lit up when discussing places like Maui. I wanted to give her everything she desired. When we made it home that evening I told her I would book a trip. Instead of being excited she flatly said we didn't have to. She thought we should be saving our money for a house, retirement and other boring adult stuff. She said she appreciated the thought and the effort, but right now was not an appropriate time for us. She could say that, but I saw how she lit up when we discussed it earlier. It crushed me, but I knew she had our best interests in mind.

How our relationship worked was so different from any previous girl I had been with. I couldn't help but compare Aida to the string of women before her, and how she stacked up in every category. There was no comparison as she won in a landslide each time. Now when I thought of Pauline, it was truly in contempt. If there was this much potential for relationships to go this well, what the hell was I doing with Pauline for even a short period of time? The question baffles me now.

I finally had a girl that I talked of the future with. We were constantly talking about our plans, our hopes, and our dreams. This was great, but sometimes caused me great anxiety. Aida had large hopes for the future. A future she deserved. She wanted to travel the world and she wanted me to go with her. She wanted to raise a family and move to the suburbs. I feared I could never provide her with such a lifestyle. Between the both of us working full time, we would be lucky to afford a decent apartment. Life was going well, but I feared what was to come. I didn't want to lose the best damn thing I had going for me.

Baillargeon

Chapter 6

Aida was out having brunch with some friends on a sunny Saturday morning, leaving me alone in the apartment. I put on the TV and flopped onto the couch and flipped through the channels.

Cartoons. Nope.

Documentary of some kind featuring the voice of none other than Morgan Freeman himself. Boring.

Some old movie with Jon Legouiziamo and Bob Hoskins. Looked stupid.

There is never anything on Saturday morning television once you pass the age of twelve. Considering the girlfriend wasn't home and I was chilling in her place, I figured it would be a suitable time to swing by my pad. I wanted to check out the old place and grab my mail.

I hadn't been back to my place in two weeks at this point. I hadn't seen or talked to my brother. I was afraid to return there. I contemplated phoning him to warn him I would be popping in. Then I realized I was warning someone that I was coming home to my own place. Seemed stupid. I decided to pop by unannounced instead.

I was trying to convince myself the place would be in decent shape and my brother would be up. It was ten o'clock. I had such high hopes for the scrawny shit. I put my key in the door and opened. The place was so dark I couldn't see a thing. That did not stop my nose from working though. It smelled of squalor. I turned on the light to see why. There were beer bottles and pizza boxes everywhere. I believe I also detected the slight smell of urine. I should have considered buying wood chips for a hamster cage and spread those before I left. In the middle of the destruction lied two full grown males, one on the couch, the other face down on the floor, hand still grasped to a PBR. Neither of them were my brother. Classy.

Past them I could see the reason for the utter darkness enveloping the room. The windows were black, covered with garbage bags. My brother was a real class act. I could not believe I hadn't received a phone call from the landlord or complaints from the neighbours. Then again, the complaints could have come in the form of letters. I wouldn't be surprised to learn he had intercepted them. I wouldn't put anything past him.

I walked over to the windows, stepping over the grotesque man on the floor, and yanked the redneck curtains from their duct tape frames. Light burst in followed by sounds of life from the two drunks. I kicked the body on the floor while shaking the man on the couch to wake them both.

"Rise and shine boys," I tried to say in a polite voice. I followed less politely with, "and I don't mean to be rude here, but get the fuck out of my house."

At this, I heard a commotion in the bedroom. At least G was now up. He stumbled out of the bedroom and helped his boys regain consciousness. He tried to be as kind as possible as he rushed them out the door and told them they would talk later. It was not the time to worry about being polite. He knew his pissed off brother when he saw him. Closing the door behind the two gentlemen, he turned to look at me, still standing shirtless in a pair of briefs.

"What the fuck G?" I asked with my arms out, palms up, twisting my body side to side. It was as if I had to show him the room for the first time.

"I know man," he said with disappointment, "things have been getting out of hand recently. I'm really sorry." He started to pick shit off the ground.

"Clean it up later," I told him. "Go get some clothes on. Let's head out for some breakfast. I can't be in here right now. Do something about this though. Today."

"I will, I promise." At this he headed back into the bedroom. He was in there longer than it takes for a man to put on some jeans and a T-shirt. After a few minutes of sitting on the couch, surveying the damage in disgust, a cute girl came out of the bedroom. Disheveled, but cute nonetheless. She didn't bother to raise her eyes or say hello. She picked up her high heels and walked out the door barefoot. It was going to be an embarrassing walk of shame for that poor girl. My brother came out of the room after she left. He now had a smile on his face, right from ear to ear.

"Burn my fucking mattress while you are at it too," I told him as we stood up and took off for breakfast.

-       -   -   -   -   -   -

We grabbed a seat at a diner around the corner. It was famous in the neighbourhood for its cheap breakfast. That was because it wasn't overly tasty or fulfilling. A small Korean family ran the restaurant. Probably not a single wage paid out to any of the six family members working in it. It was the family's money. I could almost guarantee they lived in the back as well. A common occurrence around here. How bad could anyone screw up breakfast though? So this is where G and I usually grabbed it.

G had bags under his eyes and such insufficient strength he struggled to keep his head up to be engaged with me. He was suffering through a hang-over and downed the first glass of water he had in front of him. I asked him to recap the night as I thought it could have been interesting. After he finished telling the story, I realized it wasn't.

He asked me how Aida was and how things were going between us. I had been feeling uneasy lately and I guess this opened the flood gates. I was comfortable talking to G for some reason. It doesn't make sense because I don't think he ever had any advice to help me with.

That didn't stop me from telling him everything. I was happy. I was in love with a beautiful, intelligent, funny and sexy girl. She was somehow in love with me. However, I was uncomfortable that I believed Aida could do better than me. I was always a little nervous. I had trouble understanding why she liked me so much.

I thought that I was a decent guy. I could treat Aida the way she deserved to be treated. I was only concerned I couldn't deliver on all she wanted to accomplish in life. Some of those things took money. Money I didn't have. I was constantly trying to come up with new ways to earn a few extra dollars. I figured that's where I was lacking. If I supported my girlfriend and got her everything she deserved, I would be fine. I just needed to make a few extra dollars, or cut back on expenses a bit.

"Why do you think Aida is with you anyway? How did she not have some sugar daddy taking care of her before you came along?" he asked honestly and inquisitively.

"She's not like that. And trust me, I have wondered, and asked, the same thing. She said she didn't want some asshole with money. She said she was waiting for a nice guy like me."

"Dude. There is your answer. Stop worrying. Shit will work itself out. Aida is not like that anyway. She knows you're a fucking poor ass plumber."

My brother was trying to be supportive. He had a way with words to make me feel better. However, he wasn't reading between the lines. I had been supporting him financially for some time. I was going to need to cut him loose if I had any chance of keeping myself together. I knew Aida was not going to break up with me because of money. That didn't mean I still didn't feel obligated to provide for her. If only I had enough to support myself, my girlfriend and my dumbass brother, I could have been set.

Chapter 7

My brother made an effort to be kind and he may have even been right. Yet, I had this unrelenting feeling of uneasiness. I wanted to bring it up with Aida. We generally talked about our issues, but this one was different. I felt like a failure of a man to tell her I couldn't give her what she wanted, what she deserved. Instead, I was on my own. I was spending a lot of time thinking about ways to raise extra money. I dreamed of the gifts and experiences I wanted to provide to Aida. Thinking about the ways I wanted to spend money on her, they scared me. I had no plan on how to pull it off.

One night we were lying in bed after sex. It is the time I get most confident bringing up uncomfortable subjects. Maybe my defenses are down when I am naked. Or maybe I finally have some blood flowing back into my brain. It was when I first told her I loved her. It was when I first asked her where she thought this relationship was going. I remember how pleased I was with the answer. She said she saw a long future.

As long as I didn't 'fuck it up', was her caveat. I was afraid I was already nearing that line. There had to be thoughts going through her head of what she was capable of professionally, in her relationships and her life in general.

I still sort of danced around the subject. I told her I was considering getting a side gig, maybe bartending or waiting tables. She asked why I would do that. I told her I could use the extra bit of cash. She fired back that she was afraid I would work too much, that we wouldn't have nights to hang out or do activities. I would end up having to work weekends and she wanted those available in case we wanted to take a trip or go out. She missed the fact that without the work I couldn't afford these things. I decided not to push it any further.

I was afraid of the imminent conversation that she would break up with me. I had worked it into my head that a break up was inevitable. The thought of losing her made me physically ill. My life had improved so much since meeting her. I couldn't remember what it was like without her. It scared the fucking shit out of me. I began thinking I was developing an ulcer. I was throwing Tums in my mouth like I was eating popcorn.

I was at work Monday morning when G called and asked to meet me somewhere to talk. This was a rare occasion for him to be so cryptic and wanting to meet up. Concern rushed over me thinking something was terribly wrong. He was in some kind of trouble and I was worried I wouldn't have the cash to bail him out. I told him I would meet him right after work. The rest of the work day had me in a fog, my mind racing with possibilities. I got increasingly upset thinking of the shit I have had to do for him. It was piling on. I wondered what G could have gotten himself into. I hated him at that moment for adding to my existing stress.

We met at a small pub we used to frequent together. We liked it because it was quiet, we could keep to ourselves, drink for cheap and sometimes shoot pool. It was quiet because it was a dank old place with a long skinny bar. The floor was carpeted as many establishments were back in the 70s, and years of booze and self-loathing had soaked in to give off a unique smell. In the back there were a couple of booths surrounding the pool table. The few people that came in generally sat at the bar, alone. As I walked in a few heads rose to see the newcomer. When they saw I was going to add no further entertainment to them in their day, they went back to their business of doing nothing. I could see G was already at the back by himself, sitting in a booth with a beer in front of him. This also made me nervous, as he was never early. Not even for an activity he arranged. I grabbed a beer from the bartender and made my way to G.

I sat down and he started by making small talk. I cut him off immediately.

"What did you call for G? You got me kind of nervous here. Let's cut to the chase."

"Well, the other day you were telling me you were uncomfortable with your financial situation. Lord knows I need to start bringing in some money myself." He maneuvered his position in his seat and leaned towards me.

"We both know a lot of people right? And people trust us, right?"

"You mean they trust me," I broke into his spiel.

"I can be trusted you fucking dick," he snapped back loudly enough for the five or six people at the bar to hear and briefly look in our direction.

He calmed down and continued as everyone's head slunk back down into their drinks at the bar. Their excitement for the afternoon was over.

"So I was talking to a bunch of buddies and they were saying how much of a pain in the ass it was to get weed these days. You have to buy it from some fucking douchebag. Guys whose homes have a katana hanging over their couch. You remember that guy Alan who used to require us to go through the front door and his mom would let us in?"

"So you want us to be those douchebags?" I kind of laughed when I realized where he was going with this.

"I think we can do it without being douchebags."

G drew out his plan to start selling. He listed the people we know that smoke and how much they smoke. Sadly, this number was depressingly high (no pun intended). With them alone we could provide enough to pad our pockets.

"And where, do you suppose, are you going to get that much of a continuous supply?" I asked.

Of course he knew a guy that could provide drugs on demand. This is where I got nervous. I didn't know this guy and whether or not he deserved our trust. Was I going to be able to put my trust in my brother? I gave it serious consideration.

Pot was illegal and the selling of pot could put me in jail. The prospect of jail had never sat well with me. I assume it does not sit well for anyone. However, how does one end up in jail? Every pot dealer I knew was retarded and they made money and stayed out of trouble. How could I not pull it off? I was complaining to my brother about how I needed some extra income. This was one way I could get it. I wasn't sure how Aida would feel about it, but maybe she didn't have to know. If for some reason I did get into some trouble, it would be best for her not to know. Plausible deniability. I had heard that on political shows. It's just weed. Weed never hurt anybody.

I started to think it could work. If I was going to do it, I had some concerns and some stipulations we had to cover. My brother needed me, my contacts, and I would guess, my money. I felt like I was in control.

One of the stipulations I had was that G would have to get an actual job. Selling this shit wasn't a career. It was a way to add extra coin into the pocket. The minute he treated it as his way of making money is when he would get in trouble. It is damn suspicious for an unemployed stoner to be flush with cash. If we were going to do this, I was going to take the opportunity to get G in a real job. Not the best motivation to do so, but whatever works.

I had one hundred percent control of the operation. However, I would be a silent partner from the purchasing. The guy doesn't know about me and G handles him completely.

We only sell to people we know and trust.

We don't skimp, skim, or try to rip anyone off.

We pay for any smoking we do ourselves as if we were normal paying customers. I didn't want G getting him and his friends high constantly off our stash.

I saw, and was responsible for, all the cash.

G had no problems with any of these. I told him I was going to have to sleep on it. We would talk about it more the next day.

Chapter 8

I dreamed of selling weed throughout the night. It was one of those dreams where I was still wide awake. Like day dreaming, yet I didn't have control of how things were playing out. The story was taking care of itself. It wasn't a nightmare, so it couldn't have been the worst idea. I was dreaming about providing drugs to a group of friends and how it would work. I was going over the math in my head that my brother had proposed. He had listed the people we knew well enough to sell to. He was right. Every one of those people would start buying off of us if it was an option. The connection for supply was the biggest issue and if G trusted the man and was going to take the burden of risk, I couldn't see any big issues. I was positive there was no chance we would ever run into the law. By the time morning rolled around, I hadn't slept, but I had made up my mind. I was going to provide an innocent plant that has never hurt anyone to my friends for a fee. I was going to be an intermediary between two parties. I wasn't going to be a drug dealer.

I went to work the next morning and the anticipation built during the day. There were things I thought we would have to prepare. Ziploc bags and a weigh scale turned out to be it. I decided we would hold off a week or two so we could start telling our potential clients. I didn't want to get a massive bag to find out everyone I knew had already bought, meanwhile my shit was drying out.

There were a few concerns which I thought they were insignificant. I believed there was no chance we would get in trouble with the police. I didn't think they cared about pot. People had been smoking it openly in the park. I would hear people get in worse trouble for smoking cigarettes. My biggest concern was that selling would get annoying. I didn't want potheads calling me at all hours, demanding ridiculous things or hanging around too often. I've seen it with other people. Most customers would be my friends anyway, so I was hoping that wouldn't be an issue. The other concern was Aida. I had no idea what I was going to do about Aida. How was she going to feel about this? I was planning on figuring that out at a later date. I was doing this for us anyway.

After work I phoned G. I didn't offer any hello. Just an, "I'm in." It felt like the cool way to do it. That's how they would do it in the movies.

G was ecstatic.

I had to talk him down and explain the new details I had come up with during my sleepless night. We wouldn't be up and running for another week or two and I would delay that further if he didn't get a job. I was real serious about that issue. Aside from that, I was ready to start making some tax free coin.

We were going to be paying a thousand bucks every two weeks for a half of a pound at a time. Cash was tight when I paid for the first stash. I was nervous getting it, but I can say that my heart rate picked up and a rush came over me to be holding that giant bag. I had never held that much weed at once before. The odd guy I bought off of would have bags like this, but he would divvy it up in front of me.

Now that it was in my possession, I just wanted to hold it. G and I were like giddy school girls. Turns out I could still be immature. We took turns grabbing it, hugging it, breathing it in. To be fair, it was a giant bag to me at the time.

We did have a plan to follow though, so we busted the bag up into many smaller bags for distribution. It was smiles and jokes the whole time. The plan was in motion. We were doing this. Once we saw how many smaller bags it made, we got concerned about moving that quantity of product. I didn't want to lose any money on this deal. In the end, it did not take long to make my money back. Then the profits rolled in.

We had talked to a bunch of friends, and they were keen on getting product from us. It alleviated our apprehensions to see them stay true to their word. We delivered some to their places, and some people swung by the apartment to pick some up. We didn't have to negotiate about money, everyone paid, and we were well on our way to make this a successful opportunity.

After we had sold the entire load, we were sitting on around 2,500 bucks. G was disappointed with the first round of sales as I paid myself back my initial thousand dollar investment. Another grand had to buy the new bag, and we split five hundred bucks profit. Two hundred and fifty bucks was not exactly what G was expecting. After the second bag though, he understood. We split 1,500 every two weeks, seven hundred and fifty bucks each. The extra 1,500 a month tax free was going to help me out big time. The problem was G wanted more. It was tough to keep him in check. He knew this was my operation though. I think he was well aware that if I left him to his own devices he would end up in trouble, broke, or in jail. Possibly all three.

We sold most our stuff in quarter ounces. The odd eighth every once in a while if they weren't heavy smokers. Those were my contacts. Most of G's friends were big pot heads so he had less stops to make to get rid of his share.

At first I didn't tell Aida. I was going to keep it a secret. This lasted around five weeks. I had to lie to her to keep the secret. It left me feeling dirty. I justified it because I thought it was in her best interest. I had decided I was going to tell her, but things came to a head before I had the chance.

I had been spending a lot of time at my own place during those first couple weeks. It was easier, as that is where G held everything and we measured out bags. I was at Aida's one night watching some TV when I got a text from a buddy looking for a hookup. I was going to have to make a delivery. My house was now where we stored the goods so I would have to run home. I told Aida I was going to visit my brother. It wasn't bad because I wasn't really lying, or at least that was how I justified it to myself when I lied right to her face. I only omitted the fact that I would be delivering someone an illegal substance afterwards.

I was getting my shoes on to leave when I looked up to see a look of sadness on her face. Tears built in her eyes.

"What's wrong?" I asked, genuinely concerned.

My heart broke thinking she was that sad for a reason I was not aware of.

"Are you cheating on me?" she asked.

She was sitting on the couch staring at the floor. She slowly raised her head up to meet my eyes, her tears starting to flow in full force. Panic struck as I swiftly moved back to her and sat on the couch to put my arms around her.

"Where the hell did that come from?"

She went off. Quickly rattling off a laundry list of suspicious activity. It was clear she had been building this up inside of her. I had no idea. I had been so busy lately, I hadn't noticed what I was doing to my poor peach.

I had been staying at home way more often than before. I would suddenly have plans out of nowhere. I would leave her in the middle of activities or shows we were watching.

Then the big one. I had been protective of my phone and not letting her see my texts.

I had been careful not to leave my phone out. I had changed it so it would no longer show a preview of the text on the screen when I received one. When I got a message I knew was related to dealing, I would generally leave the room or angle myself away from her.

No wonder she thought I was texting girls. I was an idiot.

When she told me these things, I saw it all. It crushed me to think she thought I was capable of such a thing. I would never do anything to deliberately hurt her. I had to tell her. So I told her everything. How it came up, how we were doing it, who we were selling to, and finally, why I did it.

"Why would you think you have to sell drugs for me to stay with you? I have never once thought I needed more than you already give me. I love you, you asshole. Don't you get that?"

"I know," I told her, admittedly defeated.

"It's just that we both want so much out of life and I'm afraid we can't get it at our current pace. With this, I have been putting away extra cash. Cash we can use to do so much with our future."

"It can't come at the cost of your freedom."

"It won't. I have covered the angles. I am being safe."

"But it's illegal."

"What's the big deal? It's a plant. It's not a dangerous drug. I wouldn't be hurting anyone. People are going to get their weed no matter what. What is the harm if it's me, a trusted friend that gets it for them? One could argue it is safer they are getting it from me. Not only can they trust the stuff (Hell, I smoke it myself to ensure its quality and its unadulterated excellence), but the money is not going to some two bit criminal who will probably invest the money in his other nefarious activities. I want to raise money so you and I can live comfortably. Happily ever after if you will. What better reasoning is there?"

I paused for a minute. She didn't seem convinced so I kept going.

"Not to mention I am finally going to help my brother. He was going to do this without me. If he did, he could have messed it up and gotten in trouble. This way I will give him some direction and some ability to make it on his own. I was the one who forced him to get a job, otherwise I wouldn't help him with this. Now he is working and has to take something seriously. If G could learn a few lessons, he will be much better off in the long run."

I waited again. Finally she spoke.

"You know how I feel about marijuana, I have no problem with it whatsoever. I do have a problem with breaking the law though, even if I think the law is silly. There are so many cons, I don't know if they outweigh the pros."

We debated this subject for some time. It was hard for her to be upset about it as we both agreed it should be legal. It is such a harmless drug. There were still risks that could cost us, but every one she could think of, I had a rebuttal for. In the end, she understood. However, she sounded overwhelmed, and I could tell she was still angry.

"I trust you will not do anything to hurt us. If you think you can make some extra money without any risks, I don't approve, and I don't think it's necessary, but I won't stop you. I believe you are too smart to get yourself caught. What I can't allow to happen, is you lying to me. You have been a real asshole these last couple weeks, and you aren't going to simply get away with that. You owe me big time."

"I am so sorry. That was completely inconsiderate of me. I didn't think I had changed much. Now that you explain it, I see how it could have looked. That was dumb of me. I love you, and I would never do anything to hurt you," I told her.

"I know, just be careful."

This is where I needed to stop and think. I had thought of every possible angle and prevented a lot of risks of getting caught. I should have been thinking of other possibilities aside from getting caught, but now that Aida was aware of the situation, I felt invincible.

I still had to get going to drop off a quarter for my buddy Adam. This time I wouldn't be lying to Aida about where I was going and I would come back to her house instead of going home for the night. There was still plenty to hash out. She had thought I was cheating. But after a few hours of clearing the air, the sex was fucking fantastic.

Baillargeon

Chapter 9

The first few months of selling were getting to be kind of fun. Once we got into the groove of things, and I was no longer lying to Aida, there were a lot of perks you would never think of when being an intermediary of weed. There was the obvious advantage of having extra money. We weren't making a pile or anything. Although after a few months we were hitting our target of two ounces a week with no issues. It wasn't difficult. By the time our two weeks were up we were generally dry, needing a new stash. I sent G to meet his guy every time with explicit instructions. Nothing too serious. Don't get too involved with the guy, keep your visit short and make sure we will still be ready to go in two weeks. Sometimes product got tight and if he had to cut back we wanted him to do it to his other guys. I always finished with reminding G to never speak to him about me or the business we do. The only thing he needed to know was we could afford to keep paying him.

I hadn't spent a dime I had made on the venture so the cash was adding up. I hid it where nobody could find it. I would never tell a soul where it was. I wasn't quite sure what I was going to do with it. Watching it grow had me feeling butterflies in my stomach every time I counted it. I would feel this way, regardless if the cash you get is sometimes terrible. It looked like a pile of old newspapers and trash. You wouldn't want to lie in it like they do in cartoons. You could catch a disease or some kind of bacteria. It was usually low denomination, sometimes it was petty change, and the cash was generally crumpled and dirty. I dished out most of the terrible stuff to G and held on to the better cash myself. He wasn't upset. He thought all that coin would come in handy.

Aside from the money, some of the folks we sold to were fun and interesting people. We generally knew them well. Sometimes we didn't keep in touch like we should so the connection had been lost. This gave us an excuse to see them on a consistent basis. I don't know why I lost touch with some of these folks. They were fun to be around. On top of that, some of them held some sweet gigs. Being their intermediary had some perks.

I don't know another business such as this one. I provided them a product at a profit. I did it because I made money, yet people treat me differently from other retailers because my product was weed. I got benefits from my customers that I don't believe their grocers, liquor store owners or other retailers got from them.

I had four bouncers at popular places that now bought from me. This almost guaranteed me immediate access to some of the hottest clubs in town. At other places I simply needed to drop one of their names to get in. They had a tight bouncers' network. My guess is they worked out at the same gym. That or they got their steroids from the same guy. It must have been a pre-requisite to be unnaturally bulgy to work at some of these clubs. Either way, because I sold them illegal substances, I was admitted to their secret society.

I was being given tickets to events, brought to some awesome parties, and treated like everyone's best friend. These were friends, but some I didn't see often and suddenly I was their bestie. They would do anything to make sure I liked them. Aida and I were royalty.

The regular Joes I delivered to sometimes provided a good time or a good laugh too. Bringing them weed got to be funny to see the different types of people and how they handled their smoking. Some were so secretive. I wasn't allowed to come by when their girlfriends were home, because they were unaware they were closet stoners. What a terrible way to live. Others would light a joint in the middle of the park and not bother to do an obligatory shoulder check. Some kid would be walking by with their mother. I don't think pot is that big of a deal, but I liked to show some respect in public.

There were a couple of old friends that had kids a few years ago I got to see. Something about having kids and settling down. You don't see your party friends anymore. I went to my buddy Adam's place often and his boy was always around. He was almost four years old. When I gave his dad a baggy, he gawked at the small bag and asked his dad what it was.

"It's medicine for daddy. It helps daddy and it's not for young boys. If you want to grow up big and strong like daddy, you will stay away from daddy's medicine, okay?"

"So he is a doctor?" the kid asked while pointing up at me.

"Ya. I guess you could call him that," he replied while staring at me with a big smile on his face.

I was far from a doctor. Maybe a pharmacist. People struggle with the distinction and I didn't think a four year old would get the explanation, so I let it slide.

It was nice to see these guys, even in this context. I did find it weird though. I know I was just an intermediary of drugs, but when I have kids I would never be seen like that. It still was interesting to see from this side of the equation.

The other big advantage was G finally took my advice. He actually got a job waiting tables at a local pub. Turns out it was perfect for him and for our side business. He was doing well at the job and people liked him there. The manager was fond of him and was already training him to work behind the bar. G also loved the attention from the women he worked with.

He had an instant in when they found out how easy it could be for them to score bud. You would think his manager would not appreciate him slinging pot at his establishment, but the man was taking a quarter off us every week. He was awesome to both of us. As my brother worked the bar tending gig, my girl and I hit it up often to show support. We would sit at the bar and drink our faces off and the manager wouldn't charge us a dime. I hoped these people didn't expect favours back. My stuff was never free. I couldn't afford it.

Baillargeon

Chapter 10

Drug dealing was good. That didn't mean it was perfect. The more we got into it, the more problems that arose.

Customers were continually trying to introduce us to new people. They enjoyed our service, our product and our company. Eventually, they would tell their friends. No matter how many times we told them to stop, it kept happening. It was an okay problem to have, people liking us. However, we weren't looking to grow our business. I didn't like the idea of new clients who were once removed from the friends we knew and trusted. Without knowing them we would be opening ourselves up to risk and that was what we were trying to avoid. Still, they were introducing me to new groups and it was awkward. It was the kind of introduction where they said things like 'this is that guy I mentioned' or they say my name and raise their eyebrows a couple times. They continued to do this as if I didn't understand. They were talking about me when I wasn't around.

These new introductions seemed great, and it's nice to meet new faces. I just didn't want my only trait to be known for as being a hookup for marijuana. It made me feel cheap. I had so many other qualities to offer to these people I called friends. This is what rich assholes must feel like. Or why we assume they are assholes. I wasn't sure if they laughed when I talked because what I said was funny or they were trying hard to impress me.

With all this happening, and knowing I was more financially secure, we partied harder and more often. The weekends were write-offs and the odd weekday drunk made for some difficult work days. I want to say my work didn't suffer, but I had some days where I puked in the sinks I was working on. Luckily I didn't get any complaints back at the office. I was still doing my job but the party scene was taking its toll. I had to keep myself in check to not let bad habits get control over me. My career was being a plumber. I couldn't forget that. Both Aida and I were enjoying ourselves so much though. We partied at the hottest clubs. We had a few celebrity run-ins too. I won't mention any names, but I thank God I didn't let Aida have a list of three celebrities she could sleep with. She had a shot with at least one of them.

I was also delivering most of the product I was moving. I didn't want customers coming to my home. I wanted the option of leaving instead of having to kick people out of my place. Potheads have a tendency to linger. Between my regular work hours, distribution and parties, I was starting to wear thin. On almost every visit, they wanted to burn at least one with you. I was smoking way too much grass those days, and if I was having that problem, G was probably turning green.

I began to feel partied out. My body was beginning to reject me. The invites kept rolling in and I hated saying no. I got worried if I said no, they would stop asking. Some nights I was down and out on the couch, sometimes hungover, and it took a lot of energy to pull myself off the couch when a new friend invited me out. A couple Redbull Vodkas and I was generally back in the game, but my hangover was intensified the next day. I was pushing them off until I would finally spend a day dead to the world. Aida was not impressed at what she called my Deferred Delirium Tremens or DDTs. Made sense considering it felt like someone had dropped me on my head.

We had to make a few small changes.

After some serious discussions we got G's manager at the bar to take over the selling to his staff. He had to promise not to sell to customers. If people started talking about how his establishment was a place to score shit, that kind of word gets out and brings heat we didn't want. He was an upstanding guy, and though I only knew him for a few months, I believed him to be trustworthy.

I decided I couldn't do the standard deliveries anymore. The last one that finally brought me to the decision wasn't too bad. It was that they were such time wasters.

I had walked into my buddy Mike's place and had a seat on the couch. After my last encounter selling to someone with a child, I found it increasingly weird to sell drugs to someone with kids. Mike was a closer friend and smart guy with his life in order, so I couldn't help but ask, "What are you going to tell your kids about marijuana Mike? They will start to wonder."

"I dunno. I'll deal with that when the day comes I guess. That's the problem with weed, I don't have to think about it when I'm high," he chuckled.

Seems irresponsible, but I think he said that for my benefit as a joke and he took his parenting seriously.

Mike was already busting up a nugget and rolling a joint. He was going to be disappointed when I told him I was rolling out. I had to move things along. I was about to ask him for the money he owed (they always start rolling before they hand you that) when there was a rattling in a cage next to a couch. I jumped back when I saw it. "What the fuck is that?"

Mike laughed. "That, my friend, is a hedgehog. I picked it up a few days ago. My kid has been asking for a puppy, for like, forever, and there is no way I am getting him one while living in this tiny shit box. Last year I told him it was too much work and I would get him a goldfish instead to teach him responsibility. Well I'll be damned if that little nine year old isn't the best damn caretaker I've ever seen. Loves that fucking goldfish. I haven't touched it and that damn thing won't die. I thought about murdering it several times to try get myself out of the situation. The kid insists he is ready for a dog."

"Father of the year Mike," I interrupted.

"Ha ha, don't I know it. Last week he kept telling me how much he deserved a dog and I didn't know what to do. I went down to the pet store and thought I would get him a gerbil to tie him over for a while. Well, the sales guy convinced me these hedgehogs are way cooler and more fun. So I thought I would try something different. Doesn't he look cool?"

"I guess, but for some reason I don't think your plan is going to work. I have a feeling a hedgehog is going to get boring. Hedgehogs can't be good business. On that note, neither can not getting paid. I need my money Mike. I gotta get running."

"You aren't sticking around for a quick puff?" he asked like a disappointed toddler. He took some cash from his pocket and handed it to me.

"Good luck with the hedgehog Mike." I slapped him on the shoulder and made my way to the door. "For future reference, anything less than an ounce, I won't be making house calls anymore. I am getting pretty busy and I gotta get some time with the GF. We can chat about it next time when you need your next hookup. See ya around Mike." I said as I walked out the door.

Mike gave me a hard time. He wanted me to stick around. It wasn't often his wife and kid were out of the house. He was pulling out every peer pressure trick in the book. I have a rubber arm, so it was not easy for me to say no. I had to start standing my ground. Aida was waiting for me. I told him I was sorry but I had to go.

I heard some muffled reply as the door closed behind me. Turns out being friendly with your client is not as enjoyable as it sounds. It would be better off if they were strangers. This had become a full time job.

If I wasn't delivering the product myself I could rely on G and maybe one or two of my best customers. Maybe growing the business wouldn't be the worst thing. Remove myself from the risk and make additional money. It sounded easy. Although, I wasn't convinced it was the best idea. I would end up overlooking some angle. I was not a criminal mastermind, I was a fucking plumber.

At the moment, I was doing as much business as I needed to. One of the hardest things is keeping yourself in check. It is too easy. I couldn't let the situation get away from me. It was time to get my priorities back in check. I had to focus harder on work so I didn't get in trouble with the boss. I had built up a lot of goodwill there and I couldn't wreck it. I had to keep G on the straight and narrow. He was doing well. Lastly, but most importantly, I needed Aida to know she was number one to me. I couldn't do anything stupid to ruin our relationship.

Chapter 11

It was Friday night and my brother had invited us out earlier in the week. We were preparing for our evening and getting dolled up for the occasion. Aida dressed to impress and was looking damn fine. She already spurned my sexual advances on numerous occasions as she was getting ready. She hated when I did that, which was often.

"What is on the agenda tonight anyway?" she asked.

"I am not exactly sure," I replied. I wasn't. G hadn't told me what we were up to. He told me this group of friends were a lot of fun, were partying this weekend and he wanted us to join. I was hoping they weren't a bunch of assholes. G sometimes gave too much credit to some people. 'Nice' people meant boring, 'fun' meant crazy, and 'hot chicks' meant whores. I had gotten used to his definitions of characters.

Aida began giving me her regular riot act.

"Well as long as you know I have to be back at a reasonable hour tonight. I have things I have to do tomorrow so I won't be able to stay out too late. If you end up getting loaded or this is looking like it will be a runaway, I may attempt to bail on you."

I knew there was no changing her mind on this.

"I'll take it easy too then. We will come home at a decent hour."

"Ha! We will see about that. I love you honey, but your self-control while partying is to be laughed at. You will forget that comment by the time someone orders the first round of shots. By the second round you will be buying the third and fourth, so let's be honest with ourselves okay?"

I wished she was joking. That was a standard night out for me. I have poor self-control with alcohol. I decided not to fight her on the issue and defend myself. I didn't want her to throw the retort in my face tomorrow morning if it did in fact happen.

We got to the bar and G had secured a large corner booth. It was a trendy place. The kind that spends a fortune on how to use enough fixtures to barely light a place. The furniture was brand new and looked like trendy IKEA shit. Everything was blocky and wooden. We had these couches wrapping around the corner with a few stools around the table. G had ten people there already.

My brother ran through everyone's name in the room in order from left to right but skipped the guy in the middle. At the time, I hoped it wasn't because he was black. I got concerned it came off as racist. I knew that couldn't have been the case. My brother was a lot of things, but he wasn't racist.

When he made it through everyone he came back to the guy and introduced him as Jam. Everyone called him that because he was Jamaican. Not exactly a clever nickname. At least now I saw the reason behind the skipped introduction. He was important in some way. My brother obviously liked the guy and wanted me to meet him. I reached over the table and shook his hand. He grabbed my hand firm and stared me straight in the eye. A respectable shake is a rare find.

"Nice ta meet you mon," he said with a thick Jamaican accent.

He was a tall skinny bastard, and at the risk of sounding racist myself now, the most stereotypical Jamaican I had ever met. He had a dark complexion with dreads down to his waist. His head was covered by one of those knitted hats. I wondered if he was high, drinking Malibu, and I would have loved to hear him talk of the Jamaican bobsled team (Cool Runnings being the majority of my Jamaican knowledge).

Either way, he was genuine and carried a smile from ear to ear. He looked like he could be one of the nicest people at the table. I introduced myself and Aida to everyone else one more time. I like to lock down the names. We ordered some pints to get going.

I loved hanging out with Aida in these situations. We were both comfortable in working the room together or on our own. She was as adventurous talking to other people as I was, so neither of us had to babysit the other when out in public. We both had a few drinks and carried our own conversation. I sometimes caught myself watching Aida do her thing, she was so at ease talking to people. I was not such a natural. I had developed a system over the years of questions and tactics to start conversations with new people. To start with, I began with the regular pleasantries:

"What do you do?"

"Where are you from originally?" (Few people were from here.)

"What keeps you busy when you're not working?"

I was listening to answers and asking a bunch of questions. People love talking about themselves. Luckily for me I actually find it interesting. Some people are cool, some people are fucked up. Both are fun to talk to. During this time I try my best to bust out one-liners and get a laugh from them. The more I have to drink, the more risqué my jokes become. I am constantly testing the waters. I know when I cross the line I would have a gentle squeeze of my forearm from Aida. Depending on how drunk I am will determine how well I take the hint.

I had talked to a lot of people at the table at this point but still hadn't had a chance to talk with Jam. I was now at one side of the booth and he was at the other. When Aida got up to go use the restroom, I took this as my opportunity to switch seats.

I took an open spot next to Jam. He smiled politely and I returned the gesture. He was wearing a button up light shirt as if he was at the beach. It was the middle of winter. Must have been a culture thing. His top buttons were not done up and I couldn't help but look at his chiseled bare chest that peaked out from underneath. Jam clearly would have no problem with the ladies. He was handsome and had an athletic build.

I started with some small talk, like how he knew my brother through a random connection, who he knew in the group and the condition of the bar we were in. Then I went with the standard questions and his answers were nowhere near standard.

"What do you do Jam?"

"What do I not do mon? I am a student of dee world. I travel, I write, I create."

"Sounds like too much fun," I responded to his vague answer. "So does that pay the bills?"

"I ave enough chedda to make myself appy. What you do brudda?"

"I'm a plumber." No matter how long I have been doing it, for some reason that always stung to say. At least I told the truth. Most guys called themselves tradesman, or contractors. Lying to themselves.

"I am sure dat could be interestin." Nobody knew how to respond either.

"It can be some days. It is good to work with your hands and meet a variety of people. I met Aida through work, so it can't be too bad." That was the best justification of them all.

"So where are you from originally?" I changed the subject.

"You may ave guessed, but if not, I am from Jamaica mon."

"I was positive your accent was Scottish," I responded sarcastically, "I was way off. So where in Jamaica are you from?"

"If I told you, would you know? Ave you been to Jamaica?" he asked back.

His comments could have been sincere or he was trying to be a dick at this point, so I played along.

"Well I have never been, but I know that Kingston is the largest city and capital. I know a few names of the tourist type places too. I have read a few articles, you know, the Wikipedia entry. Curious about where you come from or what brought you here," I defended myself.

"No worries mon. I am in fact from Montego Bay. Tourist country. I dealt wit Americans all dee time. I was tired of living off dere money, decided I could come eere and make it on my own. Left my family behind and tryin to make a name for myself eva since."

I continued asking him about what that entailed as Aida returned and joined me talking to Jam. The uneasiness I had at the start of our conversation dissipated as I got to know the man. He was the most interesting guy I could ever remember meeting. I wish I had half the adventures under my belt that he had. He did as he pleased. It was as though he wandered through life aimlessly, but had no problem with that. He was just living. Aida liked him as well. He paid compliments to the both of us for how we were together, especially out in public. He said we were a 'power couple'.

"What about you Jam? You have a special girl?"

"I ope so mon. She is out dare somewhere. I am patient, I will find er someday."

"There is no better city for it. No shortage of fish in this sea. With your traveling, you have intentions of living here for a while?"

"I believe so. I like dis place. I ave bought a ouse eere, so I ope I can make it my ome. When I got to dis city, it frightened me. As I got to know dee place, it grow on you. I feel as doe I could stay eere for a while."

"Now if you will excuse me brudda, I must use da facilities. I will talk to you lata. It was very nice to meet you both."

He got up and made his way to the bathroom. As he did, G came over and took his seat next to me.

He leaned over and asked, "What do you think of Jam?"

I found this evening so strange already, especially with G's man crush on this guy Jam. I responded, "He is pretty cool, but why do you have a hard-on for the guy and why are you so curious about my opinion of him?"

My brother leaned in closer and said, "They call him the Mushroom Man."

Chapter 12

The Mushroom Man was the nickname beyond the nickname bestowed upon Jam. Jam was the name they used in his presence. The Mushroom Man was what they called him when he wasn't around.

My brother told me he had met him through a buddy at a bar one night. They had hung out a couple times. One time Jam had some amazing mushrooms. They were far better than any other ones he has ever experienced and I had to try them. G filled me in on his plan he had from the beginning. He wanted to get into the mushroom trade and he believed Jam would be the guy to talk to. As he was finishing explaining this, Jam made it back to the table. I awkwardly stood up as he returned and asked G to accompany me outside.

I wanted to drive the point home. I ranted on him outside where the smokers hang out. I was quiet so we would go unheard by the others, but stern enough for G to know I was serious.

"We are not drug dealers. We are not trying to grow some empire. We are a couple of guys who could use some extra cash. We get that by providing a natural plant to a few of our closest friends and trusted acquaintances. What do we know about mushrooms? I like your enthusiasm, but let's take a step back here. You got a group of friends out there that came out to party with you. Forget about the money, our side business, any thoughts of mushrooms and let's have some fun. I don't mean to be harsh, but I don't want things to get out of hand man."

G looked dejected. He was looking at his shoes as he shuffled his feet. He was taking a moment, but I could see he understood. I may have bursted his bubble too abruptly. I wished he could be that enthusiastic in other aspects of his life. I waited another moment for a response.

"Are we cool?" I asked finally.

"Ya man. I see where you are coming from. Sorry for springing this on you like that. It was an inappropriate way of trying to bring it up. Let me grab some drinks and let's have some fun."

"Sounds good brother."

G was headstrong and normally would put up a huge fight. Sometimes, when I was stern enough, he would back down easily. This time he didn't have any fight in him. After everything we had been through, I was like his dad. He listened.

It was a humbling feeling for me, and it was odd to be so respected by someone.

I went back to the table and sat down next to Aida. My brother followed shortly with a round of beers and a round of shots. He passed them around and the crowd cheered. This was a classic G overcorrection. He was feeling sheepish, so he bought everyone booze. The two rounds most likely cost around two hundred bucks. He shouldn't have been spending that kind of money. I figured I had scolded him enough, and he was trying to be nice, so I didn't say anything. The party was about to begin anyway. Aida doesn't do shots so when nobody was looking I had to down hers too. Things were about to get ugly. This is exactly what Aida knew was going to happen.

We got after it. At one point I wondered if maybe one of my drinks had drugs in it. It would have been hard to tell which one of the eight shots of Jäger someone could have put a drug in. There was a chance I was actually just flat out wasted. It was okay, we were having a great time. I was talking up a storm with a few people at the table, including Jam, who was the center of attention in the large group. Our table being that one in the bar that was too loud. The rest of the bar was left wondering what the hell was so funny as we erupted in laughter every couple minutes. Meanwhile, we were putting down drink, after drink, after drink.

It was getting late, but the party showed no signs of slowing down. Aida was getting concerned. There was talk of moving to a new venue instead of going home. The group was discussing where to go when Jam suggested a place he knew. He said nobody has heard of it, and that we should trust him. It would be an adventure. This was the opportunity Aida needed to pull the chute and bail from the situation. Instead of saying goodbye to everyone and taking shit for ditching, she squeezed my arm and whispered into my ear, "I'm outta here. I'll see you at home."

When she made a statement like that, there was nothing I could do. She was going home and had warned me this was going to happen. She got up as if she was going to the bathroom. Instead, she Houdini'd from the party. It wasn't until we were getting cabs that someone noticed her absence. I let them know she had already gone.

We took several cabs to an address Jam gave to everyone. I rode in the one with him. He interviewed the cab driver for the entire ride. He tried to learn his whole story in a ten minute span. Some of the details he pulled out of him in that short period of time was impressive. The cab driver looked disappointed to see him go when we arrived at our location.

We got to the address first which was for the best. Looking around, I would have had no idea where to go. I didn't see any club around. We waited for everyone to arrive so Jam could lead us to where we were going. We were downtown, but not in any district that has many bars. It was a lot darker, quieter and eerier than I was used to. During the day, it would be full of pedestrian traffic. At this hour, it was not the most inviting place. The tall structures lit up, but the street level was lacking in the comforting glow of neon signs and store front shops. We ventured halfway down an alley. I couldn't have been the only one who wondered where the fuck we were going. The darkness closed in on us and the smell of urine began to fill the air. Jam was going to get us mugged, raped, or murdered. Hopefully not all three, or at least not in that order.

We walked up to this giant metal door. It was unmarked and in the side of a giant dark brick wall. I had definitely never been to this place. It was way off the beaten path. I was nervous. Sometimes these places turned out to be fantastic hidden gems though. I could live next door to the greatest bar for years and not know it existed. You could find a new place at any time.

We walked through the first metal door and a large man with a beard that would shame a lumberjack was sitting on a stool in a small room next to another door. Jam was saying a few words to him and the big man stood up from his stool and opened the next door. As the second door opened the music became almost unbearable. It was loud enough to kill conversation. It was also dark, as the room was only lit up sporadically with lasers darting throughout the room. Didn't seem like any trendy hidden pub. It was too low tech. That's when I noticed Candy descending from the ceiling with grace. Guys whooped and hollered immediately.

Candy was a stripper. A big titted stripper sliding down a metal pole. We were at the peelers.

I was never a huge fan of the strippers. Something about them made me uncomfortable. I think it was the underlying sadness of it. I wanted to stay out with the group, so I played along. I took a seat next to Jam on perv row, the row of chairs lining the stage. As close as you can get to the dancers. You could tell Jam liked strippers as he didn't hesitate to grab his chair. We grabbed drinks and continued to chat as if there wasn't a naked girl dancing two feet from us. Jam's eyes did not leave Candy's body, then Jasmine's, then Crystal's. We chatted through his ogling of women. Jam was definitely the most interesting character at the party. He had stories from the world over. For a broke ass kid living off tips from tourists in Montego Bay, he had made a life for himself. I was jealous of him. That may be why I was so drawn to him. I wanted to learn how he did it, how he made it look so easy.

I didn't have as many interesting stories as him. I did tell him about Canadian strippers though. Canada was the one interesting place I had on him that he had never been to. In Canada they take off every piece of clothing, including the bottoms. They get their cooches right up in your face. Then they do the oddest thing. They have this thing called a loonie, a one dollar coin. It has a picture of a loon on it. They have a toonie which is two dollars with a polar bear on it. The name doesn't make sense. Sounds like someone's lazy marketing.

Anyway, they lick these coins and stick it on their breasts or near their vagina. You take a roll of your own loonies and you throw them at the girl, trying to knock the coin off their body. It's how they make their tips instead of getting bills tucked in their G-string. Jam thought this was hilarious. He swore to me he would make the trip up north to witness it.

We were so busy chatting and watching naked women that we didn't notice the party trickling out. My brother was shitfaced and struggled to speak when he tapped me on the shoulder to say he was bailing. Soon it was Jam and I, still pounding drinks and hanging out on perv row.

It was four in the morning when they said the show was ending and the lights came on. A waitress brought over our bill and Jam picked it up. I argued. I still didn't understand how he had money, but he paid the tab. I was gracious and tried to give him some cash but he refused to take it.

We walked outside and were now on the street. They say this is the city that never sleeps, but around four in the morning it can get pretty fucking quiet. The odd car was driving by. Thankfully the odd taxi was too. Before I flagged one down, Jam asked if I wanted a smoke. He pulled out a monster joint. I was far too drunk to say no to that. We smoked it and its effects quickly rolled over me.

I was floating in the clouds. My mind was swimming. It felt like I had lost my ability to do basic math, yet I was capable of understanding the intricacies of the universe. Had we begun talking it out, I am certain I would have found a way to bring peace to the Middle East.

With that going through my head, the only words I could muster out were, "Holy shit man, this stuff is amazing."

That's when it hit me. I just got higher than ever before, with a man I had just met, in a strange corner of the city, at an ungodly hour I shouldn't have been awake for.

"Um, what else is in this shit?"

"Dat, me mon, is dee purest, cleanest and best ganga that as eva been grown. I arvested it myself earlier today. I call it da Red Leaf."

"You grew this? Why is it called Red Leaf?"

"Tell you what mon. Come by me place Sunday. I will be kicking around at home. I'll show you."

He passed me a card with an address on it and turned and walked away. Just like that, I was standing there by myself. I was as high as I have ever been, in downtown Manhattan, in the middle of the night.

I couldn't have felt better.

Chapter 13

Whatever effect that joint had on me the previous night, it was gone the next morning. It was replaced by the worst hangover I have experienced. To be fair, once you hit a certain age, every new hangover is the worst one you have had. My mouth was so dry I didn't think I could open it for fear of cracking. I opened my eyes and managed to focus on the clock. Nine. Too early. Next to the clock on the end table was a giant pitcher of water. Sometimes I am proud of my drunk self. I took the pitcher in hand and guzzled its entire contents. I put my head back on the pillow and shut my eyes.

Eleven. That ability to fall back asleep saved my life that day. It was time to get up.

I was at home which was a surprise. I normally would make my way over to Aida's. She had some stuff to take care of that morning, so I'm glad I didn't bother her by crawling in sometime around five in the morning. Selfishly, I was also glad she couldn't bother me sometime around seven or eight when she got up to head out. I sat up on the couch and held my head in my hands. I tried to will my body into recovery.

G came walking out of the bedroom looking like a sack of shit. He was moping around in his underwear and shuffling his feet, seemingly unable to lift them off the ground. He was such a scrawny shit, you could confuse his thinness with being in shape. The reality was his abs popped because there was no meat on top of them. He walked right by me, unaware of my presence and judgements. I had crashed on the couch when I walked in last night and he didn't know I was there. I was watching and listening to him moan and groan with his back to me as he ran some cold water from the sink. He was about to take a drink when I announced my presence.

"Hey," I threw out there.

He jolted so hard his glass of water spilled down his bare chest. Washboard abs he would always attempt to call them.

"Jesus Christ," he yelled, "where the fuck did you come from?" He was now alert. He came over to the couch and had a seat next to me.

"I must have come home last night, I don't really remember." I was going through my phone, looking for any evidence in a couple texts I had sent last night. "I know it was sometime around five in the morning. I sent a text to Aida at 4:45 to say I was home safe. I got a little fucked up last night."

"You and me both. How bout them strippers? Hilarious place. I had no idea it existed. Jam is cool like that. He knows these things somehow."

"Ya, I chatted him up a lot last night. Good dude. We smoked a gagger at one point and I was so fucked up. I think I walked around aimlessly for like thirty minutes afterwards. Some amazing shit."

"I believe it. The man has connections. You should try the shrooms we got off him once. They made you feel like a super stud. I imagined myself a foot taller, looking down at other people. Was some trippy shit."

"Ya, I don't think I need that." We sat in silence for a moment, before I wanted to address the mushrooms he brought up once more. "About that G, sorry for freaking out on you last night. I was surprised when you sprung it on me. I know we have a pretty good thing going right now. I don't want to ruin it. It isn't worth the risk."

"Hey, I get it. It was a stupid thing to bring to you when I had invited you out for the night. I shouldn't have an agenda when we hang out. I am sorry too." He paused a minute, clearly uncomfortable. He wanted to move on. "What's your plan for the rest of the day?" G asked.

"Not sure. Nurse my wounds I guess. I'm thinking television, couch and quite possibly the fetal position sound good right about now. You?"

"Well I have to work later tonight. Any recovery I do has to happen in the next six hours. I am working behind the bar, so I want to do well. Tony is helping me out a lot, so I don't want to let him down."

"You have no idea how happy it makes me to hear you say that."

Seriously, my brother was making an effort. I know he was drunk until two or three in the morning last night, but what bartender isn't?

I was beaming with pride when my phone rang. It was Aida. She had been out with some friends that morning as she had planned. She was happy to hear I was still alive. When she asked me what I planned to do today, I told her the exact same thing I had told G. She told me to come over to her place to do that. She would take care of me. She would love a day of doing nothing also. G was not going to be getting up to much either, so I said bye and took her up on the offer.

I arrived at Aida's house and she had picked up some sodas and assorted junk foods. They were spread out across the coffee table. Every one of my favorites was there. She was in her favorite lazy clothes, some sweats and T-shirt, and sitting on the couch already. It was an inviting scene.

"Hey babe. This looks fucking fantastic."

"I thought you would like it," she replied. "Come sit. Take your clothes off if you want."

"You know I do."

I stripped down to my underwear and crawled under the blankets next to her. She sat on the end and I stretched out with my head in her lap. She stroked my hair as I told her about the rest of the evening after she had left. She was disappointed I went to the strippers without her. She would have liked to have seen the show.

She reached over me onto the coffee table and grabbed a joint. "I'm assuming you want in on this?" she asked.

"Seems like an amazing idea."

We smoked a joint together and my hangover floated away with the rest of any issues I may have had. We put on a movie and ate some munchies, wasting the day away. It was perfect. This girl knew how to treat a guy. I was thinking I was going to have to remember this day the next time she was hungover. I definitely owed her one.

When we finished our movie we remained in our horizontal position. I snuggled up to her and we laid there for another hour chatting. Eventually, she steered the conversation to how things were going in my side business. Not that she wanted to be involved in it. She was curious how things were working out. I was honest with her and we had a healthy talk. I think it gave her some relief to talk about it.

The rest of the day was as expected on a major hangover. We lied on the couch and watched several movies. We smoked a few joints and ate far too much terrible food. For someone who was a health nut, she had a soft spot for terrible snacks.

The munchies didn't help. As it got late, we fell asleep during a movie. When she woke me up we decided to give up and move to the bed. It was a complete waste of a day, and I loved every minute of it.

She was special and I was so in love with the girl. I would do anything for her. I would kill for her. I would die for her. Hopefully, it would never come to the latter.

Chapter 14

Sunday morning I woke up and snuck out of bed without Aida noticing. She had treated me so well the day before, I wanted to repay the favor. I wanted to make her breakfast in bed, so I started cooking some food. I didn't make it five minutes before she woke up to the noise and came out to see what I was up to. I had the hash browns on the go and was preparing bacon for the grill. She came up behind me and put her arms around my waist as I stood at the stove. It brought me to complete relaxation. I closed my eyes and leaned my head back onto her shoulders.

"I was going to make you breakfast in bed," I told her as she kissed my neck.

"How about you come back to bed before making me breakfast?"

That was all I needed to hear. I turned the stove off. Cooking could continue later. We made our way into the bedroom and had tossed our clothes and torn apart the bedding in a matter of seconds. Things had escalated quickly.

We laid there quietly intertwined for a few minutes and tried to regain our composure. She stroked my hair and I stared at the roof without a care in the world. Finally, she broke the silence.

"So," she began. She gazed into my eyes lying next to me naked, the blankets no longer near the bed, "Breakfast?" she asked slyly. Teasing me.

"I'll get right on that," I grinned.

She showered up and got ready as I prepared the meal. She came out glowing, telling me how she was waiting for a morning session after having to wait out my hangover recovery the day before. I was glad I could appease her. I finished up breakfast and served her at our tiny table. We rarely ate at the table. It was nice as we discussed our plans for the week. I had my visit with my new little brother and I was going to visit Jam later in the afternoon. He had invited me over. She was going to go visit Daisy and we would meet up for a late dinner. I was looking forward to it.

My new little brother was this tiny Japanese kid named Toshi. He was hilarious and I got a kick out of him. He wasn't too popular with other kids. He was into Dungeons & Dragons, reading and history. Toshi would not be fending off the ladies anytime soon, but he was super smart and insightful for his age. I learned a thing or two from him. If nothing else, I was teaching him a few social cues. He ate up pretty much anything in front of him.

-     -   -   -   -   -   -

I had received the invitation from Jam to check out why he calls his marijuana Red Leaf. I had been excited and intrigued, though I was still hung-over from the entire day prior. The things my brother had been telling me piqued my interest. This guy was mysterious. I couldn't help but want to get to know him better. I went to the address he had given me and walked up to this brownstone in Brooklyn. Like most houses in the area it was old, yet the minute you took it in, you fell in love with it. Vines were crawling up the front bricks and there were water stains down the top of the house which added character. On either side of the steps were magnificent flowers. I am not much for this type of thing to explain it well, but I knew it was impressive. There may have been four square feet of soil on either side with concrete surrounding it. It was hard to believe a guy known as the 'Mushroom Man' got to live in a place like this.

I stood in front of the house for some time. I didn't know what was I doing there. The short turn of events from two nights earlier left me standing in front of a stranger's house who I knew as either Jam or the Mushroom Man. The guy's real name was still unknown, along with my reason for being there. I had little recollection of how everything went down. I just knew I was invited and I had this address on the back of a stripper's card. I considered turning around and heading back home. I was beginning to sweat. I couldn't figure out why I found this guy so intimidating.

Then I wondered why I was so concerned. Those situations are where epic stories usually begin. I decided not to wuss out.

I walked up the few concrete steps and searched for the doorbell. There wasn't one. It had one of those old fashion knockers which I had never used before. I guess that was a first. Everything about this guy was an adventure. I took the handle from the golden lion's mouth and lifted it to produce three loud bangs on the door. I stared at the golden lion with a large intricately designed mane. It appeared to be expensive, maybe real plated gold. It scowled at me as I waited.

A few moments later Jam opened the door wide and greeted me with a big friendly hello. This caught me off guard. I don't know what I was expecting. I guess when going to check out a man's drug operation I thought something different than this. Maybe a sliding slot in the door and the use of a password like 'the ducks fly north in summer'. At least be more sly and discreet.

I walked into the house and Jam closed the door behind me. It was a beautiful, normal looking place. We entered the living room which boasted some antique furniture that worked well in the space. There was no TV, which didn't surprise me. I didn't expect Jam wasted a lot of time watching television. You could see the kitchen through numerous white archways making up a hallway lined with full bookshelves. By the bookshelf was a vintage metal spiral staircase leading you to the second floor. Jam told me to take a seat on the couches as I surveyed the living room in detail.

There were plenty of flowers displayed around the living room. I guessed we would be heading somewhere else to show me his Red Leaf operation. This looked as though he lived with his mother or his girlfriend. I was sure he had said he didn't have a girlfriend the other night. Since my memory was foggy and I didn't want to appear as though I hadn't been paying attention, I thought I would start the conversation generally.

"You have a beautiful place Jam. You live here on your own or do you have a roommate?"

"No mon. I live on my own. I like people, but I like my private place to be alone. Ow bout you? You seem to ave a beautiful gurl who was wit you on Friday. Very lucky mon. You ave a future, I can tell dees tings."

"Ya, I hope so. We are basically living together at this point. I would hope to make it official sometime in the near future, now that my brother has a job and can probably support himself."

"Ah yes, G. I like dat man. Eee seems like a straight shoota. You and im seem similar, yet so different."

"Ya, he has had a rough go. He will come out on top though. He is still young."

We continued this small talk for a while. Feeling each other out I guess, as our last visit was such a blur of booze and breasts. We reminisced about our crazy Friday night. As we did, we got to talking about the end of the evening.

"Well then you pulled out a joint the size of a rocket ship and I got so fuckin high. I think it counteracted the booze quite a bit and I was higher than I was drunk. Then my hangover yesterday was the worst thing ever," I explained to him.

"Ya mon, I ear you. I should ave sent you a Red Leaf for dee next day to get you troo. It ese a wonder drug."

"That stuff was remarkable," I admitted, "where do you come across weed like that?" I finally asked him.

"Come wit me man, I'll show you ow I do."

I headed to the door thinking we were heading out. However, he waved me over to the spiral staircase by his kitchen. We climbed up and the aroma took over. As he opened the door at the top of the stairs, the smell was overpowering. I peered in and I could only see a forest of red plants. It was borderline frightening as it looked blood red.

I could not see any of the walls beyond the plants growing in this room. It was marijuana, the smell was unmistakable. The leaves were familiar in shape, except for their color. Looking closer, the unmistakable bud was present, and still green, providing a bright contrast on the plants. Some were a few feet tall while others were starting to graze the ceiling. Hovering above were many bright lights and tubing ran above each plant, most likely irrigation hoses.

I surveyed the room with my jaw on the floor. I was blown away. I turned and faced Jam, his face was beaming and his smile was from ear to ear. His arms were crossed and he leaned back like a proud papa.

"Welcome to my shop of strange and wonderful tings."

Baillargeon

Chapter 15

"What the hell is this?" I asked.

"It is my farm mon. I ave been piecin it togedda since I moved eere. I afford it by sellin some of my mushrooms on dee side and dee odd bud when dey come in. I ave been tryin to use my experience to grow dee best plant possible."

"How is this even possible?" I was flabbergasted.

I began walking through the garden, brushing by the plants. Bud was grazing my cheeks and the aroma was powerful. I worried I could overdose by standing in the room. It made no sense, but it was intoxicating.

"I ave studied in biochemistry, cytology and dee genetics of plant structures. I took classes at Cornell for a brief period in botany to lcarn dee science be'ind it. From der I ave travelled dee world, moving from place to place, culture to culture, where a varietee of plants are grown in a varietee of environments. I learnt so much. It amazes me ow small we ave made dis world but still do not share our information. Not because we are tryin to keep secrets, but because different cultures do not care because dey tink dey know everytin. It's a crazy world my mon."

I was still walking around the room. Touching. Examining. Trying to wrap my head around it. He kept talking.

"When I came back to dee United States afta six years of travellin, I began to experiment. I ave tried many fertilizations, chemical treatments and cross breedin da best aspects from different plants. Two years of effort and it as allowed me to create dis marvel dat stands before you today."

He was speaking gibberish to me. I didn't understand a fucking word coming out of his mouth. I was more curious how he managed to have such a setup.

"So that shit's crazy, but how do you get away with this? This is a huge grow operation."

"Well I ave taken measures to ensure I don't get caught, if dat's what you are asking. I sourced everytin from multiple stores in multiple locations. I have done dee work myself, so nobodee knows dis exists, except for one guy and I truss him completely. One of dee biggest issues is dee amount of electricity I require to run dese lights." He pointed at them as if I didn't know which lights he was talking about. The things were blinding me.

"I ave a friend, an electrician dat works for dee power company. Ee has done some work in dis area. Did it before I moved in to avoid any suspicion. It's dee reason I live in dis specific ouse. Dee power dat connects to dis ouse is a combination of juice coming from dee entire city block. A large increase in power, small when it split between 30 ouses. I also installed a bunch of filters dat I found to circulate dee air in my ouse out dee roof. As you can tell mon, dis is some sticky ganja. I don't need my neighbors catchin whiffs."

"Well what happens when someone else notices? A different electrician working this area, noticing the lines not doing what they are supposed to or whatever?"

"I am not an electrician mon. I could not tell you sheet about ow it works. I can only tell you dat I ave a friend whom I trust. Ee is an electrician, and ee tells me dat I am safe."

"Jesus." I was at a loss, so I turned my attention back to the plants. "So why are the leaves red?"

"Dee red leaves are dee brain child of ingenuity and blind luck. I ave travelled and studied many different cultures of marijuana, and I took da best from dem to create dis. Dee secrets and ingredients dat lie wittin stay wit me. I show you dis because I want you to feel comfortable standing be'ind your product."

"My product?" My face must have portrayed my confusion.

"Ya mon," he stated matter of fact.

"You want me to sell your weed?"

"You sell already mon, but you sell sheet. Why not sell dee best?"

I sat there dumbfounded and searched my brain for a response. Where the hell was this coming from? How did he know I sold weed? What did he know about me? The questions were circling between my ears. I stared down at the floor as I tried to process the situation.

"Why me? You met me two days ago? How can you trust me? How can I trust you for that matter?"

"Like I said mon, I ave travelled dee world, met many people. I believe I am a good judge, and you mon, are good people. If dat wasn't enough, I ave asked around. You are well known and it's not for your sellin. You ave a steady job and a great woman. I am not in dis to make a fortune, just to share my creation wit dee world and make enough to be appy. I believe you are dee same. Because of dis, you are careful, no?"

"Well ya, but this doesn't seem that careful."

"Look mon, I ave brought you to my ome. I ave shown you my operation. I am not messing wit you. In terms of careful, I ave some ideas. We can discuss. What you tink mon?"

"I have no idea what to think man. I wasn't sure what I was expecting coming here, but I wasn't expecting this." I was staring around his farm. It was glorious. I had never seen anything like it. I doubt anyone had.

"Well mon, I can grow dee sheet. You ave tried it and I assume it is dee best you have ever ad?"

"Ya, but," he cut me off right there.

"Look mon, I can grow it. I love to grow it. I don't care about dee money dat much and I especially do not care bout avin to sell it. I am not lookin to grow any more dan I ave already. I want to keeck back, spend time workin on new tings, and ave someone else look after dee selling and dee money. Can I count on you to do dis?"

Baillargeon

Chapter 16

I didn't know what to do. Things had escalated rather quickly. I was an intermediary of marijuana to friends. This was a legitimate operation. I was not confident I could find the justification to be a part of it. I would officially be a drug dealer. Jam could see I struggled with the idea.

"Like I said mon, I am not lookin to make a fortune. I grow what I can fit into my ouse. I have split my entire upstairs into four sections. Dere are tree different settings for dee different gestation periods of dee plant. Den a section for dee arvested crops for dryin and bagging." He showed me the preparation area.

He had a small table in the corner next to a whole lot of bud hanging from a rack. It looked like seaweed. A tangled mess of green spread like a sheet. There were a couple fans running and placed around the rack, keeping air flowing by, causing the bud to swing to and fro. This was his dehumidifier. On the small table was a scale and some baggies.

Not much different than the table in my apartment where G was working. Except where I used small sandwich size, Jam had large freezer sacks. This was the big time. There was a whole row of clear Ziploc bags filled with bud lined up across the table. Next to them was a pile of smaller red, and a few green, bags. The color was hiding what was inside them. They were set aside though, as if they were special.

"What are those?" I asked, pointing at the colored bags.

"Those are dee mushrooms I grow. Dee red are 50 dollars a gram. Most people need tree grams, so 150 for high. Expensive, but almost dee best mushrooms you will evva ave. Make you feel big and strong. Dee green are a special blend. Dey are difficult to make. Dey cost 1000 a gram. Dose are dee best mushrooms you can evva ave."

My jaw dropped. "1000 a gram? What the fuck?"

"Ya mon. Dey is some amazing sheet. But I don't want to talk to you about mushrooms today. Mushrooms are my hobby. I don't grow much and it is mostly for personal use. I ave dat andled. Marijuana is my passion. As you can see I ave a smooth operation rollin eere. By my calculations I can grow and arvest a pound a week, year roun, wit a solid rotation."

"A pound a week?" I couldn't handle anymore shocks. "I don't sell half of that. I am not looking to get rich either, so this is a bit much. I don't think I can move that volume or need that much heat."

"Why would dis bring more eat? It's dee same ting, just sell a bit more," he retorted.

"You make it sound so easy. I don't sell to someone unless I trust them. And I don't mean trust them to not be cops. I need to trust them not to share or sell to someone who is retarded and could do something stupid. I do this because I make extra money and it is completely harmless. I don't hurt anybody. I don't want this to turn into something that could. That's a lot of responsibility."

"You work wit you brudda right? Maybe step back and let im andle a lot of dee face to faces. I ave a feeling you can trust im to nevva breed a word of you or drop your name to anyone."

"My brother can be trusted one hundred percent to not say a fucking word about me. Unfortunately, I cannot trust him to not get himself in trouble. I care about my brother and don't want to see him get hurt."

My brother hadn't crossed my mind yet. He would not be happy with me making any decisions like this without him. For the last two days I have scolded him for trying this exact thing. I would be sending him a terrible message if I went ahead with this. I was having trouble wrapping my head around the situation. Meanwhile, Jam kept going, forcing me to try keep up.

"Well ow bout you keep your brudda completely in dee dark. We don't need to be friends. Juss business partners.

Ideally we would set tings up and ave no more contact anyway."

We discussed the details of what this would entail. I wondered how I got myself into these situations. I wasn't sold on the idea, but I wanted to talk it out. I managed to pull my head out of my ass to examine how it could work. We would do blind drops. I would leave cash, he would leave product. We would never be in the same place at the same time.

I would pay him the same thing I pay my dealer now. Aside from the product changing, and my need to increase volume, not much should change from my end. This could bring in added money on higher volume. I would also have the benefit of selling a way better product. We talked for hours and by the end I had turned agreeable. I had let my guard down to discuss it, and Jam took advantage. I think he knew he had me.

"Let us celebrate our new partnership wit a special smoke," he said as if I had already agreed. I tried to ignore his confidence.

"A special smoke? What does that mean?"

"I will show you mon."

We made our way up to another stairwell. This one led us to the roof. On the roof were pigeon coops. Several of them. This man got more and more interesting every minute. Granted, I had not known him for many minutes. Most were spent intoxicated in some form.

"You keep pigeons too?"

"Ya mon. I love dee little rascals. Where some people see pests, I see a beautiful creature. Not to mention I like to run many experiments and dey just so appen to like gettin igh. Dee ones in dis cage are of particular interest," he said, as he made his way inside a coop.

I stood back hoping he wouldn't invite me in. Just because this was interesting did not mean I enjoyed the smell. I was also not walking into any situation in which I could be shit on.

"What makes these different than the rest?" I asked from the safety of outside the coop.

"I ave tested many different diets on deese pigeons. I ave done some chemical enhancements to dem wit an interestin side effect."

He grabs one of the pigeons and holds it firm in one hand. He grabs one of the largest feathers and plucks it from the bird, then places the bird back in its cage with care. There were scissors sitting on the corner of the cage he used to cut a piece of the feather end off. He took the feather and stuck it into what was the end of a pipe used for smoking. It had a burnt black screen in it. I could see where this was going. The bones that make up a wing are hollow and the smoke would pass through the wing. He took the fresh weed he had in his pocket and packed the bowl. He passed me the makeshift pipe ceremoniously with two hands. I was about to smoke through the wing of a pigeon.

"It is a peace pipe mon. We smoke togedda to form a bond. Let us stick to our arrangement and we both shall prosper."

I accepted the pipe and he lit the bud with a match, and I inhaled. There was definitely an odd taste. The bud was the same stuff we smoked the night before. Strong as ever. The taste was the remnants of a bird wing that I found unsettling. I was happy to see him take the pipe from me and hit it himself. I was assured I had not been poisoned. Good sign.

We sat and continued to talk details out. However, we were now high as fuck. Our conversations were now going back and forth between business and our lives. An hour later I looked at my watch and realized I needed to get going. I was so high, I was uncomfortable with the idea of leaving. The general public would have me paranoid.

"I gotta go, but shit, I am still so high," I told Jam.

He laughed loud and heavy. "Don't expect dat to stop anytime soon. Like I said mon, interestin side effects. You will be stayin dat igh for a few more ours mon. Get comfortable. Let me see you out."

Who was this guy and how did he manage to do these things? He should have been curing diseases or ending world hunger. Instead he was a pot prodigy. What a crazy world we live in. If only people had the right priorities. Meanwhile I was a fucking plumber, high as fuck. Maybe he did have the right priorities.

We got to the front door and he showed me out. He had grabbed a large bag of grass upstairs which he proceeded to hand to me at the door.

"Eere is dee first pound," he says to me.

I had still been on the fence this whole time. Now I was standing at the front door with a huge bag of marijuana in my hands. He pulled another small bag out of his pocket. A red Ziploc bag.

"Take deese mushrooms too, as a gift. Try dem out."

He passed me the bag. I stuffed both into my jacket. I was high and I found myself going along with it. I was so intimidated and enamored by him at the same time. He made it sound so easy. The extra money would help, but I wasn't positive I could do it safely. I was so high. It just kind of happened. Apparently, I was going through with the deal.

"Unfortunately, I opefully will not see you for a long time. You are an outstandin gentleman, but I need a dealer I can trust more dan a friend. Take it as a compliment mon. If you do ave to talk to me, I ope it is of dee direst situation. Avin said dat, I look forward to doin business wit you. Good luck," he said as he closed the door behind me.

For the second time in three nights, I was alone in the city after getting higher than I have ever been. This time I had a pound of grass and a bag of mushrooms under my jacket. I left a legitimate drug dealer. I was running late for my planned date night. I knew it would be hard to explain to Aida. Hell, it was difficult to rationalize it to myself.

Chapter 17

Things had happened so fast there were some aspects I hadn't thought through. First, I had to bring this to G. I spent the entire following day at work trying to think it over. Mostly, I was trying to justify it to myself. G was obviously upset when I told him I made this decision without him.

"What the hell bro? Where is this stuff coming from? What am I supposed to tell my buddy who we're getting from right now? How the hell are we supposed to move that much weight? Just the other day you were cursing me out about expanding our business. You are a fucking asshole man." He was angry and ranting on. He made a few valid points.

My first step was to roll him a joint with the Red Leaf and get him to try it. That would ease some tension.

I busted up a piece of bud from the huge bag in front of us. "Already breaking your other rules and smoking off the stash," he commented. He was pissed off. I chose to ignore this comment and carried on rolling.

I passed him the joint and a lighter, almost as if it were a peace offering, to let him light it up. He took a deep pull off the joint and held it. He was holding in a coughing spurt and his eyes were watering in his effort. Finally he exhaled and wiped his eyes clean. He knew this stuff was impressive. He passed the joint back to me for a drag. We finished smoking it in silence.

"Holy fuck man," G was high as a kite already, "this shit is fucking amazing. Why the hell do you call it Red Leaf?"

I explained everything I could. I had made a promise to Jam to keep him out of it. I intended to keep it.

"They call it Red Leaf because apparently the leaves of the plants grow red." I decided to lie and pretend like I hadn't seen the grow-op. "It's some pretty potent shit though. I don't know what we can tell your guy, but we obviously want to sell this primo stuff over his shit. I don't know if you can tell him the truth, that we have another supplier. Maybe tell him you decided to get out of the drug dealing business. Can I leave it for you to take care of?" I asked.

G was high. He was staring off into the corner as I was talking to him. He still nodded in acknowledgment.

"Now with this weight, we are going to have to step up our game I guess. We have to quadruple our business. I have made a deal that we will double it over the next month, then double it again the month after. This first month we will have to look for additional customers. We will also have to find a few people we trust to sell some extra weight for us. Maybe a few of our regulars can be trusted to take extra for cheaper and sell some off themselves. I honestly don't think we will have a problem moving this much weight, especially with how good it is. Moving it to people we like and trust may be the difficult part."

"Well, let's start by not being so fucking high while we discuss this," G said, "because I don't think I can trust myself to make smart decisions right now."

G surprised me. He was being so responsible. I was proud of him.

We decided to sit back and watch a movie instead. G said he wanted to watch a classic, so he pulled out an old cassette. I don't know where he got a VCR. There wasn't one in my place before.

"I haven't used this thing yet. Hope it works," he tells me as he is kneeling in front of the TV, prepping the movie. The screen goes black and nothing was coming on.

"Take the cartridge out, blow in it. The VCR and the cartridge. Pretty sure that will do it." He followed my instructions. This time the movie started. Classic old school shit.

"Why the hell are we about to watch a VHS anyway?"

"Sometimes," he paused, "you just gotta go retro."

We watched some trippy old movie my brother must have picked up from the pawn shop along with the VCR. I was too high to give a shit. I think the movie was awesome. It is hard to tell when you are stoned. By the time it finished I had come down from my high and I had crushed two liters of Coke and a large bag of Lays Potato Chips. My munchies always got the best of me.

"Okay. How you feeling? Should we figure out this mess I got us in?" I asked.

We sat down and planned. We had lists we were making of potential clients and pros and cons of certain actions we were looking to take. We split the list of people we needed to talk to about moving some product on their own between the two of us. We were each going to have to talk to five guys about moving extra product. These were ten people we trusted, would be the safest bet and also most excited. We chatted about details like the money, and what we would do with it. We would be bringing in a substantial amount and I didn't want G walking around in a fur coat or any other stupid purchases. After a couple of hours of discussion, we were both getting confident about moving forward with our new arrangements.

Happy with our work, we decided to burn another and watch a second VHS. It was classic cinema.

-     -   -   -   -   -   -

G had to go back to his dealer and this time tell him he was not taking another bag. Apparently he wasn't too happy about this. I hadn't considered that when talking to Jam. This guy losing a customer who took a pound a month was obviously going to make him angry. G told him we were out of the dealing business and he was going to have to deal with it. I still hadn't met this guy. G swore to me he was a buddy and was harmless and he wouldn't be a concern. He said it would fall to him to deal with it if he had issues.

Off the start, all we had to do was transition off the old stuff to the Red Leaf. The guys we were selling to trusted us and they were stoked with the increase in quality. Talking to a few guys who were keen on moving a bit of product, a small sample was all it took to convince them it was a brilliant idea.

I started picking up our weed and leaving cash for Jam just like we had planned. He left a pound in a box in an alley. He said I would know which one. There were piles of boxes next to the garbage in the alley we discussed. I was looking through them when I saw one at the bottom had a question mark written on it in marker. That was going to be it. I opened it up to find a bag of grass which I stuffed into the collapsible cooler I had brought. I took the money I had stored in the cooler, 2000 bucks, and put it in the box. Jam would be back to pick it up in a while.

The way we had figured, I wouldn't be available to make the exchange every time, and Jam didn't want to meet anyone else. It was also in neutral territory, so neither of us was too close to home. It was a quiet neighborhood, and not many homeless rooting around. The garbage men never came until late in the evening, so our marked box should be fine in the two hour span we may be exchanging. If we were to lose a transaction we would revisit this plan. There was a lot of trust involved that we wouldn't screw each other over.

I put the box back in the pile and looked up and down the back street to see if anyone could have seen. There were no windows in this particular alley, so we didn't expect anyone to ever see us working. Jam's plan appeared fine in theory, but I wasn't comfortable leaving cash in a box with no protection. I worried some bum was sleeping in those boxes for God sakes. He said that was the beauty of it. That didn't alleviate my concerns. I was going to have to trust Jam that his plan would work. I would hear from him if he was to not get a delivery. For the time being, no news was good news.

Chapter 18

The fear I had of moving that much weed dissipated in a hurry. There was definitely no issue in moving grass when it was new, exciting, and fucking potent. The issue came in vetting the new people we were selling to. We had to remain cautious. We didn't want anyone selling to the wrong people. They could sell to kids too young, people who are stupid enough to drive, or carry a large bag into the wrong place. If those people caused trouble, it could lead back to us. We had to be diligent.

Luckily our regulars started to take extra off of us. They must have enjoyed getting high for the first time again. The time when you wondered what the sensation was, and if everyone else was feeling the same way. This helped us get by those first couple weeks. We had wanted to double our sales in the first month. That was easy. The issue became doubling again the next month

We had expanded our network as far as we could. We would have to take on new clients. We contacted people from our past in roundabout ways. We stretched ourselves far enough that some happened to be people we didn't like. I even let G talk to Dubs. I couldn't do it because I worked with the guy. Plus I didn't want to deal with him. I had a feeling he smoked but I never brought it up out of fear he would want to talk about it. Apparently he was an easy convert and was ecstatic just to hang out with G. Once he tried the weed he ended up taking enough for him and three close friends. It was a big help. I was more impressed that he had three close friends.

We had been getting closer with two bouncers whose clubs we were frequenting as well. I had a discussion with them that ended well. They could sell, but the issue with them was trying to hold them back. These guys knew people. A lot of people. They made my network look small. They were way too exposed for my liking. I made them choose three people and explain to me why they would be ideal customers. There was a lot of confusion from this tactic. It took some explaining, and I almost didn't go forward with it. They so badly wanted to be involved with Red Leaf. They abided by my rules.

That was what I was learning. It wasn't about the money for these people. The profit wasn't life changing. They were just happy to be connected to Red Leaf. It guaranteed their own personal supply and would make them popular when they pulled it out at parties. They only made a few extra bucks every week, but it didn't matter. It was a status thing. This made my job way easier than expected.

Things were going well in every aspect of my life. Aida and I were doing awesome. G and I were having a blast. There was one weekend Aida had to be out of town. She was visiting a friend across the river. G and I decided to have a party night and finally do those mushrooms in the red bag Jam had given me. I hadn't done shrooms in a few years so I was nervous. They could trip a guy out. My last memories of mushrooms remained enjoyable though. They can be fun. I was excited to try them again. I had gone back to my apartment to hang out with G. I opened the bag, gave half to G and kept my half. I didn't waste any time. I tossed the contents in and forced them down my throat. I chased it down with a beer for flavor.

We headed out to the bar before they kicked in. I got increasingly anxious in anticipation. I knew it was going to be crazy. I turned giddy at the prospect of tripping balls out and about. It would be hilarious. G and I made an escape plan for the night if the high turned and it got weird. It was smart to have a backup plan when lit in public. We would meet back at the apartment.

G wanted to go to a dance club where the majority of people were on some sort of drug. This way we wouldn't stand out too much. They were either on ecstasy or MDMA. I was never a fan of either. Tough to keep your wits about you, and no adult should enjoy glow sticks that much.

It had been thirty minutes since we ingested the shrooms. They were about to kick in any minute as we walked into the dance club. The venue was massive. A wide open space like it used to be a warehouse. The place was dominated by a lower dance floor. Any chance to hang out had to be done on the balconies surrounding the main area. The dance floor bounced with sweaty bodies jumping and rubbing up on each other. The lights changed every instant, with bright flashes of changing colors. The music was so loud I couldn't converse with G. I was second guessing our idea of coming to a place like this. I wasn't a huge fan at any time. Now that I had a girlfriend at home, I wondered what I was supposed to do at a place like this.

I leaned over to G and told him it was a bad idea and we should go. He only yelled 'Cool' back. He didn't hear a word I said. He clearly enjoyed the atmosphere as he surveyed the scene in front of us. I had to focus on being a solid wingman for my brother. It was tough as the mushrooms swept over me.

My heart rate increased rapidly. Almost as if it was keeping to the beat and wanting to jump out of my chest to join the dance floor. I began to notice how the lights were moving to the music, dancing with it. The people in front of me were turning into a parade passing by, everyone interesting in their own right. It was like they couldn't see me, not while I was in a different world. It gave me an understanding of the appeal of the bar. The mushrooms were starting to fuck with me.

These particular shrooms had a different effect than what I remembered from my previous experiences. They had me feeling gigantic, as if I had grown two feet and could look down upon the entire bar. I was the most confident man in the place at the moment, that was a guarantee. Old feelings of my tough guy persona I had repressed for so long were coming to the surface. I was strutting around as if to dare anyone to mess with me. I felt like I could have taken on an army platoon. There was an added effect which made it feel like time was slowing. This only served to make me even more confident. Had a prolific UFC fighter or boxer bumped into me and looked at me slightly crooked, I wouldn't have thought twice.

G and I walked right through the dance floor to the bar on the other side. I was invincible. My shoulders plowed their way through the crowd and opened a space for G to follow behind. We stood in line at the bar and I confided in G.

"I am tripping balls man. In an incredible way. I feel magnificent, like I could take on the world."

"I know what you mean. I was telling you, these things will make you feel ten feet tall. Try to maintain composure," he yelled at the top of his lungs.

G had no interest in moving or picking up women that evening, which suited me just fine. I spent the next three hours people watching. I felt like they were there just for me. I watched and contemplated life. If I ever felt like I was getting old and it was depressing me, I would have to return to one of these clubs. I watched these young people and didn't envy them in the least. They acted like children. I was happy to have grown out of this, to be with Aida. The prospect of grinding up on any of these girls was disgusting to me. I longed to have Aida there with me.

We eventually left to walk the streets. It was far too much to handle in there for any longer. Secretly, I was hoping to stumble across some street thugs or a mugging. I wanted to come in as the hero and save the day. It had been almost ten years since I had gotten in a fight. I was amped and ready to go. Not towards anyone though, only someone who deserved it. Those mushrooms were twisting me around. My adrenaline had not been that revved up in a long time.

When we got home I crashed hard. It had been a good evening. Not too eventful, but I hadn't done a day like that in a long time. It was fun to try it out. I was worried they were too good. You could see how someone would want to keep taking those mushrooms. I had to avoid temptation and lay off them.

I would settle for my pot business.

Chapter 19

Red Leaf was gaining a reputation. It was, by far, the best herb in the city. Gone were the days of people talking about Canadian or Jamaican grass. The only word out there was about Red Leaf. I had even saw a few graffiti tags showing up in some alleys. Either that or some proud Canadians were tagging the maple leaf around town. Although I think they would be too polite. 'That could devalue the building eh?'

I should have been nervous there was so much attention drawn to a product I was selling. Red Leaf made a legit name for itself. People in our network we assumed to be tight, were obviously talking. Word was out, and interest in Red Leaf was not appropriate for anonymity. It didn't bother me as much as it should have. I was too filled with pride. Everyone knew we existed. Nobody knew who we were.

I realize this pride was dangerous, but I got blinded by the fame of it. It wasn't the money. When I walked the streets, though nobody around me knew it, I felt like a big deal. All of a sudden I could see the appeal, why criminals try too hard, get too big. It's not the money. It's the pride.

Not that we didn't want the money. It turned out my regulars had realized the monetary value of my product. They were definitely buying extra these days. I thought it was because they were smoking more. Maybe they were having fun with the new strain and sharing with friends. How else was everyone finding out about Red Leaf? Turned out an entire distribution channel was setting up below us. We were selling this stuff at our standard fifty dollars for an eighth of an ounce. My buddies/customers were busting it up. Some of them were adding moisture weight or mixing it with standard stuff. Then they would sell it off to new people. This stuff was in such demand that they were selling joints at ten dollars a pop. My naivety and my pride had gotten in the way. I was so pumped about being popular, I was unaware of how much this strain of pot could go for. I was leaving money on the table. Jam had given me the same price I was paying my previous dealer so it didn't occur to me to raise the price of this product. I was a fucking amateur.

My brother was getting pressure to bring increased weight in and at that time we could keep up with demand. However, it was getting ridiculous. If there was so much demand and other people were making money out of it, we were going to have to react. It was simple economics. If supply is low, and demand is high, price needs to increase. The pricing strategy was going to need some tweaking. It was time to gouge those potheads.

I thought I would have to ease people into the situation. My only experience with price increases was through work. In the plumbing business we told our regular customers at least three months before a price increase. That way they could take advantage of any work needing to be done before it came into effect. People felt like they were getting a deal at the current hourly rate. Then they prepared for the price increase. It was surprising how well they would take the increase after. This was how I learned to do business, so it's what I proposed to G. G set me straight.

We weren't a regular business. We were selling a product and we were running short on supply. If they wanted it, they would have to buy it at a higher price. We discussed what would be a reasonable price for some time. Most of the people we were selling to I would have considered my friends. I didn't want to gouge them too. G didn't think it was gouging. It was the market price. He was convincing. He can be pretty damn smart when he applies himself. He used the words equilibrium price at one point. He had to have done some research online before our discussion. We decided on a fifty percent increase on our bags.

I thought people would be choked. When I went to my first delivery after we had made our decision, I hadn't told them of the price increase yet. I was just going to ask for it when I got there. It was quite a bit more money too. I thought there was no way this would go well. G told me to stick to the fact we would be able to sell it elsewhere. It wasn't a lie. We wouldn't struggle to get rid of any of it at this point. We didn't want to lose our current customers and have to find new ones either.

I stammered through my explanation to my first buddy. I was uncomfortable and almost shameful so I stared at the floor sitting on his couch. I danced around it until I finally spit it out. He didn't flinch when I mentioned it. He literally only said, "Dude, I understand. This shit is the shit."

That was that. Tough sale. I portrayed more confidence with my next pitches.

Only one of my guys balked at the price. At that point my confidence was up as everyone else didn't have any issues. I told him I would hang on to it, another friend was asking me for some and I would sell it to him. He caved immediately.

This weed was way better than I could have imagined. When you smoked it, it would remind you of the first time you got high. When your heart would beat so fast you thought it may leap out of your chest. Then you imagined exactly that happening and you giggled to yourself for a full minute. All the fun without the full blown paranoia some people get from smoking too much.

The business was so easy when you had the best product. I was now making more money and I hadn't spent any of it. I was living off my regular salary from my actual job. My day to day job of plumbing was going fine, but it did make me wonder about the necessity of it. With the extra money coming in and no issues, I pushed those thoughts down every time I had them.

It was about time I took advantage of my situation. What started off as a shoe box of cash had turned into a briefcase full. There were probably better ways to keep money safe. A briefcase full of drug cash though? It was awesome.

Doing the math, once I got going, I was going to be pulling in approximately $25,000 a year, tax free. I could get used to that. Especially this easy money. I didn't fear the police in the slightest. We had been careful and I had a trustworthy group of people surrounding me. Aida was being supportive of me too. She hadn't asked too much about it. She knew I was selling more, but she stayed in the dark when it came to the day to day activities. I don't think she wanted to know. That was fine by me. The venture was going smoothly. There was nothing for her to worry about. It was time for us to celebrate. I had done this for her after all.

Baillargeon

Chapter 20

I decided to finally spend a small portion of the extra money I was bringing in. As it was meant to, it was going to be on Aida. I wanted to take her to dinner and a show. I kept the details of our evening a secret and only told her she had to dress nice. I would take care of the rest. She was uncomfortable being in the dark and relinquishing so much power to me. Yet I could tell it excited her.

We decided to have our date night on a Thursday to leave our weekend plans open. I made a reservation at one of the poshest restaurants I could find near Broadway. I brought her to a small and private dining experience serving the fanciest Italian food in the area. We received the best service you can get. It was almost over the top. I felt uncomfortable having someone place a napkin in my lap for me.

I was getting used to guys fawning over my girlfriend from time to time. She was hot. This particular server was completely in love with her. From the moment we sat down, you could see how he focused his attention solely in her direction. He did not treat me with much respect at the beginning. I think guys are hoping I turn out to be a loser or a jerk. They want to think they have a chance, or to tell themselves the girl wouldn't be their type anyway. At least that is what I used to do. Since he spent additional time at our table, the waiter talked to both of us and he fell in love with me as well. By the end, he bragged about how awesome it was to serve the two of us and how much he enjoyed our company. He pulled a complete one eighty on me. We received a free bottle of wine and a free dessert. Shit like this didn't happen to me before Aida. She had this attraction about her people loved. Not just hot, but beautiful.

The food was impressive and it started our night out perfectly. We had to move on as I had lots of plans for us. I told her we would go for a walk and watch the tourists who were gawking around on Broadway. We both cracked jokes as tourists rubber necked their way through the streets.

Having grown up in Manhattan, it was weird I had never seen a Broadway show. They had never interested me. I didn't want to waste my money on one. However, Aida loved Broadway and I had not taken her before. She had been talking about this particular show for weeks. We were passing the theatre and I stopped her outside. I reached into my pocket to pull out two tickets. She giggled like a school girl and threw her arms around me. It felt so good to make her happy.

She loved the show, and I have to admit, I didn't hate it. The singing, the dancing, the theatrics, it was much better than I had anticipated. They even got me to burst out laughing on a couple of occasions. I could see myself trying some additional shows. I was growing as a human being. Becoming cultured.

We stopped off for a quick drink after to discuss the show and chat. She had to gloat, rubbing in how much I liked it, regardless of how much I was trying to hold back how I did. I didn't want her to say 'I told you so'.

We didn't last long at drinks. Aida was a bottle of wine and a couple drinks in already. I think she appreciated the night. She kept looking at me with lustful eyes. She leaned over and whispered into my ear.

"I want to take you home, and make your fucking day."

I paid the cheque.

The morning after, we still had to go to work for another day before the weekend began. Aida and I shared a romantic goodbye at the door of her apartment and went our separate ways. She was still swooning from the expertly executed date night. I had bought some goodwill for a while.

It was an easy day. I was thinking of how lucky I was to be with such an awesome girl. I was looking forward to getting home as we were going to have a night in. Aida would have to wait a while. I had a few errands to run after work.

I had to make a few drops to some buddies and then head to the grocery store for a few items. I was strolling down the sidewalk towards a group of guys walking towards me. They were standing abreast taking up the entire path. I got annoyed by people not having common sense on proper sidewalk etiquette. I decided if they were not going to file into a single line on their side, I was going to walk right through them. I looked up to make eye contact with the guy standing in the middle and he was already looking right at me. This was not coincidental eye contact. There was intent behind it. I began searching my memory for where I might have met this guy because it appeared as though he might try to talk to me. I gave a quick scan over him to try and figure it out.

There was no way I had met this douchebag before. If I had, I would have remembered him. First off, he was a ginger. I never forget someone with red hair. Especially when he had the bushiest eyebrows I've ever seen. They looked like two mustaches migrated north of his eyes. He was also wearing a leather jacket with metal spikes and studs across the back. Not the typical wardrobe of people I willingly meet or hang out with. I was thinking I maybe did a job in his house before, but he doesn't look like the type to bother fixing a leak. Even if I did a job for his mom, he would have been in the basement listening to his Skrillex. There was no way I knew him.

This made my resolve to walk right through this group stronger, keeping my shoulders tight. As I approached them I maneuvered to work through a hole between Skrillex and one of his companions. This leather jacket wearing ginger sidestepped to stand directly in front of me.

I was not about to get mugged by this petty street gang. Granted, this guy was big. He had seen the inside of a gym, and more likely, himself in the mirror at the gym a lot. He had taken his share of pricks in the ass too. I don't know if he was gay, he might be, but he was definitely on steroids.

He eyeballed me and said, "Sup? I heard you hang around this area."

The only thing I could muster up was a puzzled look as I met his eyes. Finally I managed to stammer out, "Do I know you?"

The guy stared me down and I got increasingly uncomfortable. It was broad daylight. The middle of the afternoon and people were walking the streets. A few had found their way past us, staggering around this awkward group standing in the middle of the sidewalk. They didn't notice how weird the whole situation was. I doubted I was about to get stabbed or beaten up, but you never know.

I waited for the guy to speak while his goons stood behind him trying to look tough. There at least three Affliction shirts and two Tap-Out shirts worn among them. There were fewer skulls in the average graveyard than on their collection of t-shirts. Surprisingly more brains though. They looked like Italians. I am confident these guys dreamed of working for the mafia. It was a shame they were likely too dumb. It was sad they settled for this ginger fuck. A discredit to our heritage, too stereotypical.

"You may not recognize me, but you know who I am."

He was one of those fucking guys. Thinks he is a big deal. He tells me his name. It is never worth repeating. He was just a *big oaf with stupid eyebrow rings*. His name sounded like a nickname he gave himself. It sounded like it would better suit his fat lazy pit bull he probably had at home. I still had no idea who this fuck was.

"Sorry man. I don't know who you are but I am positive we have no business together. I'm going to head out on my way if you don't mind."

"Oh, but I do mind," he replied, as he put his hand to my chest when I made a move to walk by. "For you see, you may not know me, but I know you. At first I ignored your operation. I know you and your brother were selling a little weed to friends and acquaintances. Nothing I needed to concern myself about. Now, something has come up and we need to discuss it."

My eyes were darting around the group as he kept talking, trying to get a read on the situation. With everything he had just said to me, he had now grabbed my attention and my eyes focused solely on his. I was standing rigidly in front of him at a loss for words, continuing to listen to his diatribe.

"You stopped buying. That, I originally could ignore. I got told you were out of the dope business. A man has a right to change vocations if he so chooses. Then I find out you haven't stopped selling, you changed product. Strike one. Then you get the nerve to try sell my guy some of your new fucking dope. Well that is just bat shit crazy. Strike two. However, I did have a try at it," he paused for a moment and his mouth curled into an awkward smile, "and it was fantastic. You have got yourself some fine cheeba my friend. So much so, you have managed to raise your price substantially and people are willing to pay it. They want, and are hunting down, your so called 'Red Leaf' over any standard product. Strike three. Now this gets my attention. Enough so that I took time out of my busy schedule to come and talk to you face to face. I want you to understand the seriousness of this situation. I am going to have to ask you where you got it."

Now it was official. I had no idea what was going on and the situation confused me. We were standing in the street and people were everywhere. The swarms of people rushed around us. I wanted to look around to see if someone else was as baffled at this as I was. Who the fuck was this guy? The situation was going to require some thought and tact.

"Fuck you," I told him.

Not a great plan. It didn't seem that bad at the time either.

"Come on now buddy. I have come to you, I have been polite, and I ask you this so we can maybe become friends. Is this how you treat your friends? Tell you what, since you don't know who I am, I am going to give you one week from today. October 31st. Cool? Halloween. How exciting."

This guy was weird. He was clearly insane, but he tried to hide it beneath a veneer of creepy friendliness and eccentricity. He continued talking.

"One week from today I will have some of my guys come and talk to you. In the meantime, you can ask around. Talk to your supplier and maybe you will come to your senses."

Just like that he nodded his head and walked passed. His gang of goombas followed him while bumping my shoulders as they walked past. I believe they were trying to be intimidating. I felt like jumping the last one right then and there and leaving his face looking like one of their fucked up skull t-shirts. It would have been a poor decision, so I stood there dumbfounded instead.

I was going to have to talk to my brother. For some reason I thought he may have caused this, or at least he could explain what was happening. My night at home with Aida was going to have to wait.

Chapter 21

"I am sorry, you know." G was trailing off. His head was down looking at his feet. "When we first sold Red Leaf we had that extra weight to move. I didn't know how we were going to move four pounds a month at the time. I went to go tell my buddy we would no longer be taking the half pound off him every two weeks. I told him we were done selling. He was disappointed. After the first two weeks of trying to get rid of the first pound I didn't think I was going to be able to do it. I thought, who better to move weight than the guy who already moves a lot of weight? I went back to him, told him I had got a hold of some new stuff. I gave him a small sample bag and told him to give it a shot. Maybe he would want to take some serious weight off us and we wouldn't have any issues. I honestly thought I was helping."

"You don't think your buddy has a supplier, and that guy has a supplier, and when something like that happens they don't get pissed? Come on. Use your fucking head!" I had lost my cool. "How did it come to me anyway? Why didn't this guy come to you?" I wondered.

G was still staring at the ground in shock. He did not look too hot. Looked like shit actually. He should have. I already knew it was his fault. I needed to hear how he fucked it up.

"Look, I had never mentioned you. Not ever. Like you told me. When I went there trying to sell him the Red Leaf, he had questions. Questions I didn't have answers to because you were keeping me in the dark."

"Don't you fucking dare try putting this on me," I interrupted.

"I'm not. I'm just saying, I thought he was showing some interest in buying the stuff so I had to tell him something. I mentioned that I have a brother and he is taking care of the supply. They must have checked into you. I swear I didn't tell him anything else."

"Well fuck. Now what?" I asked, not knowing where we were going to go with this. "What do you know of this ginger douchebag?"

"Just the rumours that go around. He is the kingpin. You hear about him though nobody sees him. For you to have talked to him must be a big deal because nobody knows where he even lives. He is the biggest drug dealer in the city."

"These are details I should have known earlier." I stated to G. In reality, I had been stupid myself. I didn't bother to look into where the drugs were coming from when G was getting them. They obviously had to trickle down from somewhere. That's the weird part of the drug world. You only think of the guy you are buying off of. You forget there are probably ten layers of people above him. All responsible to the next just like any large corporation. This guy was the CEO.

"So is this guy dangerous?" I asked.

"You hear rumours and shit. You don't know what's real and what's not."

"Well I need some better info G. What do you hear?" I asked. I was getting to the end of my rope with G and his bullshit.

"The rumours say he is crazy and does some pretty wacko shit. He has fucked some people up. He is supposedly a big fucking dude."

"I can attest to that. Looked like a roid monkey. I am still confident I could kick his ass, but he surrounded himself with other big roid monkeys. If he was alone I would have painted the sidewalk with his face."

I was starting to get angry. My hands clenched into fists and it took a lot of strength to not punch a hole through my own wall.

I calmed myself down and decided I needed to go see Jam to talk to him about this. I had sworn to him I would never show up at his door unexpectedly. I didn't know what else to do. This was not a possibility we had discussed. I told my brother not to mention a word of this to anyone. I would deal with it. I left him there to think about what he had done.

I hadn't seen Jam in a couple months now with the dead drops. I was nervous about how he would take me showing up at his front door, considering we had discussed it to be against the rules. These were special circumstances. I didn't have a phone number or anything for him, so this was my only option. I hoped he was home.

I didn't want to take the threats too seriously. For all I knew, it was complete bullshit and I was wasting my time. That didn't stop me from feeling uneasy and taking precautions that I wasn't being followed. My paranoia had me doubling back and jumping on trains at the last moment. I was shoulder checking the whole way. I had confidence I was alone when I walked up to the house and rapped the lions mouth on his front door. Three hard knocks on the door and I stood on his front porch. The gravity of the situation sank in. I became nervous and sweaty. Jam came to the door with a big smile on his face and welcomed me with a loud voice and a smile. It alleviated a lot of my anxiety to have this warm welcome while arriving at his house uninvited.

"Ey mon. Happy to see you," as he ushered me through the door.

As the door closed behind me his demeanour changed immediately. He did not invite me in or offer me a seat. I was standing in the entrance and he no longer had a smile on his face. He was staring right through me. It wasn't starting well.

"So mon, what you doin eere? You know dis is not what we discussed." His pronunciation was harsh and his words were cut and hard.

Any comfort I had ten seconds ago evaporated in an instant. "I know, I know. I am sorry. Something came up and I needed to bring it to you. I wouldn't be here if it wasn't important."

"Dis betta be good," he told me.

I went over the whole situation as it had unfolded to me. Jam listened and did not ask any questions or interrupt me at any time. Once I completed I had to ask him flat out.

"So I think the guy is after Red Leaf. I don't know if he wants to know who you are so you can grow for him, or if he wants to be taught how you do it or what, but that is what he is asking of me. I just need to know what you think. He says he is going to come and talk to me next week, on Halloween." I waited with bated breath. With what I knew of Jam, I knew what the answer would be.

"What dee shit mon?" He finally blurted out. "Dis is exactly what I did not want. I refuse to work for any buddy. I am my own mon. I don't want to expand. I don't want to give away what I ave worked my life for."

You could see it started with anger. It was turning to sadness and grief. I felt awful for the situation I was putting him into. I was only thinking of myself until now. He had gone quiet in contemplation.

"So," I let that linger for a moment as we both knew what was coming, "what do you want me to do?"

"Ee can not ave my sheet. No way. You tell dat mudda fucka it is not for sale. I grow what I grow, and dat is it."

"And if that answer is insufficient?"

"Den ee can go fuck imself. I leave dat up to you to andle. Do not, I repeat mon, do not give up who or where I am."

"You know you can trust me Jam. I will keep this shit under wraps I promise."

I had to leave. There was nothing I was going to say to change his mind. I knew this wouldn't be the end of it though. I didn't think I would be able to say no to this guy and that would be it. I would have to play the cards as they got dealt to me.

I needed to get home. Aida was waiting for me for our quiet night at home together. I thought maybe that was what I needed. Relax and move on like nothing had happened. I was potentially over reacting. What could go wrong?

Chapter 22

A week came and went. My mind was preoccupied most of the time, wondering what was going to become of my side operation. I went through the motions of the work week. I was hardly present. Was there any threat of violence from this ginger douchebag? Was I going to have to fight my way out of this? Maybe I would have to give up Jam. Was that an option after so many times of me telling him it wasn't? What about just taking off if it came down to it? I thought my mom would take me in. Moving to Canada was an option. I promised Aida nothing bad would come from the dealing. I doubt she would have felt good about a surprise move to Canada. My mother hadn't met her yet. The uncertainties were haunting me my entire week.

I had been so careful. We had attempted to mitigate the risk of getting caught by the police. I had not seen this angle coming. I was going to have to protect Aida from my concerns. I wasn't telling her anything about it, so it had to be business as usual at home. I didn't want her to worry about it. It may have been for selfish reasons. I didn't want her to freak out. It was a delicate situation as I was not exactly living a clean life at the moment. I worried for my own freedom if things got out of hand.

The week was painful. I put on a show for Aida and pretended like I wasn't thinking about this one issue constantly. It was difficult to act. Halloween approached and fell on the Friday. I was going to have to party it up after work to avoid suspicion. Had I tried to stay in, she would have been trying to figure out what was wrong with me.

Like every Halloween, I procrastinated too much getting a costume. With a drug kingpin threatening me, I was even more unprepared. It was five o'clock and I had just finished work. I had somewhere to be at six and I had no ideas and no materials. Going out without a costume made you look like a dick that was too cool to get involved in the party so I had to improvise. Since my improvisation skills were poor, I went out dressed like a plumber. I knew Aida would call me lazy. Everyone else would believe it to be a legitimate costume. That was enough for me.

I wore a uniform at my job. It was part of our marketing. We had red denim overalls. This was for one reason only. Everyone knows the common stereotype with plumbers, you see the crack of their ass as they worked under your sink. My boss started his company up with the slogan 'We will fix your plumbing without showing you ours'. It was printed on the back of our overalls and was surprisingly effective. Most people knew us by that line alone. It was the reason Aida called us. Lucky me. We also had red caps with our logo on the front and I kept some tools on my belt just to give it a legit look for the costume. The tools were real and expensive, so I had to be careful with them. If nothing else, I had one joke in my arsenal for the night. With a pipe wrench in hand, I could say I was getting ready to lay some pipe.

Since my costume came together effortlessly, I still had an hour to spare. I smoked a quick joint to try and calm my nerves. I had not smoked since running into the ginger. I was trying to keep a clear head. Now that the deadline of his ultimatum had arrived, I was too stressed. It calmed me down. It helped me believe I had been overreacting. I took a long stroll instead of a cab to get to the party at the bar.

I walked passed a long line of colorful characters at the front door. I introduced myself to the doorman and he pulled the rope letting me walk straight in. One of my bouncer buddies had hooked us up. Everyone was in costume. There were no slouches at this party. People were decked out in amazing outfits. It was only seven o'clock and the bar was already getting hammered. I walked around looking for the group I was meeting. The first person I saw was Aida. She was sitting at the table looking more beautiful than ever. She dressed like a princess. A sexy seductive princess. She looked fucking hot.

Wearing a tiara with her hair down, she wore a pink dress with silky material that hugged all the right places. The right places to me meant very few places. She had decided to finally join the Halloween trend of girls going more provocative every year.

She knew how to turn me on. I loved seeing her sit there, unaware I had arrived yet, watching her. It gave me a thrill to know I would be the envy of almost every guy in the bar, maybe other than the guy dressed as Elton John. That costume did not look like a stretch for him. Much like mine, it was probably already hanging in his closet.

I walked over to my girlfriend and gave her a long passionate kiss. I let my lips linger on hers to let her know how sexy she looked and to let the other guys in the bar see me mark my territory. She was taken aback by my rare public display of affection and repaid me with a smile that caused me to blush. I took a seat next to her and ordered a beer to kick off the evening.

It was a typical Halloween party night. People were getting shitfaced. One of the worst offenders was Daisy. Her behavior was getting embarrassing by eight o'clock. Dubs hadn't even got there yet. Aida decided she would have to take her home. She told me to stay and hang out as she was going to have to take care of Daisy for a while. I would also have to wait for Dubs to get there. Just great.

After thirty minutes and a few drinks, Dubs made it down. Some dinner with a family member had gone long. I had to explain to him what happened to Daisy. He decided he would just hang out with me and my friends if Aida had it under control. I advised him it was a bad idea. I had to persuade him to go home and take care of his girlfriend. Leave me the fuck alone. It took some convincing, but after a couple beers and a phone call from a sick Daisy, he decided it would be best to go to her aid.

With Aida gone, I thought I should head home myself. However, it was the best I felt in a week. I was surrounded by friends and the vibe was intoxicating. More intoxicating was the alcohol. The later the night got, the more I thought it was a big bluff anyway. Nobody was coming see me. As midnight approached, I considered myself done with it. The more I thought about it, the less it made sense. I was just a 'citizen'. They wouldn't want to hurt me. I was not a 'player'. It wouldn't be right. That was how it worked on television.

I partied until around one in the morning at the bar. I had been texting with Aida most of the night to see how she was doing with Daisy. Dubs had come and taken her place so she had gone home and wanted me to join her. I liked the idea and decided to ditch the party.

I took off and thought I could make the walk home instead of getting a cab. I wondered if I should have been worried about the threats I received, but it was past the deadline. Between that and the evening's booze intake, fears were subsiding. I strolled home without a care in the world

It was an interesting walk as there were a lot of costumes out and about. Some were quite funny. One guy was walking down the street in just a pair of jeans. No shoes, no shirt, nothing. He was with a group of people so he couldn't have just been homeless. I was curious, so I asked what he was supposed to be.

"I am a premature ejaculator," he tells me. He waited for me to think about it a moment as I didn't get it. "I just came in my jeans," he finished the joke. I had a laugh. It was clever, but he was probably freezing. That joke probably got tiring after telling it a hundred times too.

Costumes continued to walk by. Super heroes, villains and the odd guy in drag that made you question his sexuality. Which is fine as long as it didn't make me question mine. Some could look confusingly sexy.

I continued people watching as four ninja turtles approached me. They stopped on the sidewalk in front of me, blocking off the entire sidewalk. This was disturbingly familiar.

"Excuse me Mikey," I said to the orange one as I tried to slink by.

"Not so fast," Leonardo said.

Raphael held his three fingered hand up to stop me from walking by.

If this was some Halloween skit, I wasn't getting it. I tried joking with them.

"The one time of year you guys are on surface and nobody questions you hey? Good times turtles." No reaction.

"I'm trying to get home so if you will just excuse me," I tried to walk by again but was still held up by a green three fingered mitten.

"We were sent to talk to you. Now that we have some alone time, I think we should have a chat." Leonardo had established himself as the leader. Made sense.

Realizing what was happening, my tone had to change. "Your boss didn't want to come see me himself or what?" I paused but nobody was flinching. "And what if I got nothing for you huh?"

My temperature rose and my heart rate increased. I tried to keep my nervousness hidden, but I had no idea where this was going. I had been replaying this scenario for a week straight in my head. I opened with some of the questions I had thought of.

"What if I don't know anything?" I repeated.

"We don't believe you," he snapped back.

"What if I refuse to tell you?"

"Then we will have to beat the shit out of you," he was growing agitated.

"What would that accomplish?"

"Enough beatings and you will tell us what we want to know I guess. We were told to come back with your connection, or beat the shit out of you. Luckily for you, you get to make the decision on which one it is. So which is it going to be?"

These guys were not the brightest but they sure got to the point. They made it sound like a simple business transaction. I didn't like either of my options. I offered them a third that crossed my mind.

"And what happens if I beat the shit out of you guys?"

They laughed at this. These four were idiots in bulky turtle costumes. I doubted their papier-mache half shells offered the protection the cartoons had. Their limited range of motion would give me a distinct advantage. I didn't think it was funny.

I weighed my choices. If I told them about Jam I would be screwing over my business, screwing over Jam and just caving like a chump. My pride did not like that one. I could stay and fight. If I took a beating I would be in limbo again wondering where that would go, waiting for the next one. If I happened to come out on top in the fight, I can almost guarantee they would come back soon and in greater numbers. None of these options were ideal. There was only one left. I hoped they didn't know exactly where Aida lived.

I bolted. Turns out they saw that coming. They were hot on my heels. However, the papier-mache was causing them issues as expected. I was outrunning them, but not by enough. I was half drunk and my lungs and legs were failing me early in the chase. It didn't help I was wearing a full tool belt. It was bouncing around as my thighs slapped the tools around.

I had been walking home down a quiet side street so I turned the corner and brought the chase onto a main road. I was hoping to get lost in a crowd. It was late and it wasn't busy enough. The turtles were still right behind me. I didn't think I was going to win the stamina race. I had to try losing them. I saw a hotel coming up with a doorman out front so the doors would still be open. I ran right by him and he yelled after me. I sped by so fast he could do nothing about it. The four turtles plowed through him and crashed through the front door, hitting the floor. I took a brief moment to look around the vintage boutique hotel lobby. It had been around a long time. Updates and renovations made it look fancy and expensive. Not his usual clientele, the front desk clerk stared at me with confusion as I was clearly flustered, scanning the room. I saw the door for the stairs. My brain didn't reason with it. It saw an option and I made for the door.

I kept climbing stairs, all the while wondering where I was planning to go with this. I should have been trying to come up with a plan. Instead, I proceeded to run up the stairs as fast I could. They were in the stairway following me. The only thought I could conjure up was how stupid this was to further corner myself. I hit a dead end when I hit the roof access door after five floors. I ran at full speed and put my weight into the door to barrel through it. I hope that door was locked. Otherwise I destroyed my shoulder and crushed every one of my vital organs for nothing. With little breath left in my lungs, I picked myself off the floor (or roof or whatever, not sure how it works). I scanned around for somewhere to run or hide. I could hear their footsteps still coming up the stairs. Aside from a few vents, there was nowhere to go. The neighboring building was at least twelve stories taller. The hotel was on a corner so I peered over the other side to the pavement below. I didn't think I could survive the leap. These guys needed to teach me a lesson, but I would come out of it alive. Jumping was out. I ran to the front of the building and was peering down when the four turtles made it through the roof entrance.

Leonardo was trying to talk, but he was right out of breath. "Come on man.......don't make this........anymore difficult......" he stated between gasps.

I took another peak over the edge at the front of the building. I was thinking I could make it. I was pretty confident, but I wondered if it was worth the risk. I turned and faced the turtles and walked towards them. I didn't like that they had weapons. A fight could have ended bloody. Then again, those sais may be a plastic part of the costume. The sword just may have been a handle sticking out. The police would grab a guy with a sword walking around town. Nobody even knows how to use nun chucks. The bo staff looked legit though. A long stick would be an effective weapon, especially against my short pipe wrench. Walking towards them, I thought I was about to attempt to fight them. Looking at the four of them standing on a rooftop, I had a quick change of heart.

I turned and ran towards the front of the building. In a full sprint I planted one foot on the ledge and I launched myself towards the flag pole at the entrance. Grabbing the pole below the flag, I hung on for my life. As I was sliding down the pole I laughed to myself and thought I was pretty damn funny when I yelled, "So long fuckers!"

The four turtles ran to the edge and peered over to see me sliding down the pole. At that moment I went from being proud of myself to deep concern in a heartbeat. I immediately recalled a story from my early teen years.

A kid from my school had climbed on the roof of our school and attempted this very thing. He jumped off a building and rode the flag pole down. The problem was he had forgotten to think of the hooks that are commonly on the bottom of flag poles. The ones the rope ties to after running the flag up the pole. His scrotum had caught the hook and resulted in a lost testicle and more stitches than anyone ever wants near their penis. The answer to which is one. One is too many. With that in mind, I neared the bottom and I pushed off the pole. I landed with a thud on the red carpeted pavement in front the hotel. For the second time in the last five minutes I destroyed a limb while simultaneously compressing my internal organs. This time vertically instead of horizontally.

The bellman probably shit his pants when I landed in front of him. He rushed to me and helped me to my feet. He was frantic and asking me questions in a loud and hysterical fashion. I didn't have time for this as I knew the four turtles would be rushing back down. Instead I said, "Taxi," and took out a twenty which I shook into his hand. He looked at me confused and asked if I wanted an ambulance instead. I repeated my original request. He had one flagged in ten seconds and I threw myself in and was on my way. I was going to be sore tomorrow, but my limbs, and more importantly my testicles, were still operational.

Chapter 23

I got to the apartment and crawled into bed next to my girlfriend. She cooed when I snuggled up behind her. My body ached. The strain of the chase coursed through my body. It had exhausted me. When she turned and kissed me, I knew I would have to play through the pain. She had looked damned fine that evening and I hadn't forgotten. It got awkward, as getting out of overalls always is. Trying to maintain a shred of romance while taking overalls off is impossible. Once I managed to remove them she proceeded to kiss my whole body. For a girl who had already been asleep this evening, she was incredibly into this. We had sex without a word uttered between us until it was over. After, I held her in my arms and told her I loved her. She caressed my chest and said it back. Moments like this, my problems washed away. I had a beautiful girl I loved, who loved me just as much. I was the luckiest man alive.

I woke up in the morning with a slight hangover. That was nothing compared to the aches from my chase, the fall, then passionate love making. I needed a shower to get clean and assess my injuries. After washing up and poking and prodding the tender areas, I diagnosed myself with light bruising and tenderness that would fade in a few days. I hopped out of the shower and lathered on some shaving cream to get a clean shave in. Aida hollered at me from the bedroom.

"Enjoy your last full shave for a month. Today is the first of November and I believe you need to start growing that hideous thing."

Due to recent events I hadn't thought about the Movember thing. G had got everyone on board. I would have preferred to forget about it this year as it was the last thing I needed to worry about, but I hadn't told Aida about my recent issues. I didn't want to alarm her so I couldn't show any red flags. I reluctantly obliged.

I was still going to have to operate as if nothing was wrong. We had a nice lazy Saturday where we did not stray far from the couch. She knew something was up, but I played it off as nothing. Part of the hangover. I was thinking about the previous night. I had written them off, but I could see now. Those guys meant business. I would have to come up with some sort of plan. My self-appointed 'civilian status' was not going to prevent me from getting shit kicked.

I doubted they knew where I was when I stayed with Aida, otherwise they would have found me there. The fact that they only found me after midnight made me think they were out looking for me all evening. I had to lay low, not go to my usual spots, but still keep myself busy to not worry Aida. The situation was definitely fucked up, but it was nothing I couldn't handle. I believed it was best to keep her in the dark until the situation blew over. I was starting to think the worst case was that I would have to bail from the drug business altogether. I could maybe take a beating for it. Nothing I hadn't experienced before.

I thought about it constantly while continuing my regular routine. Sunday was traditional stuff. I talked to my mother on the phone for fifteen minutes. She was unaware of the crazy activities that had been going on in my and G's lives. She hadn't met Aida and I couldn't convince her to fly back home for a few days. G and I had told her we weren't coming to Calgary for Thanksgiving that year. We were too busy with our side operation. I thought that would get her to come home. I was wrong. It had been a couple weeks since then. I think she was sour over it. She kept her conversation with me curt and shorter than normal.

I was still doing my Big Brother thing and I couldn't ditch on that responsibility, no matter what else was happening. Aida was so proud of me for doing it so I had to keep it up.

I had a pleasant visit with Toshi, my other little brother, that afternoon. I had met his mother the previous week and she really took a liking to me. I had earned her trust. I had asked if I could take Toshi off the island to take him to a go-kart track.

He needed to try something sportier and out of his comfort zone. It was one of my favorite activities as a kid. This was going above and beyond for the program. I cared for the kid and wanted to do a special outing for him. His mother was excited at the idea. I had to turn down the money she kept trying to give me to pick up the tab for the karts. I had to refuse multiple times as she shoved it at me. They didn't have a lot of money and there was no way I could make her pay for what I wanted to do with him.

We had a fun time and he thoroughly enjoyed himself. He embraced it whole heartedly and giggled the entire time he got to drive. It was amazing to see the smile it put on his face. Selfishly, I was proud of myself for doing this for him.

On the drive home we chatted about how school was going. There were some bullies that were taking advantage of him. I told him of my own troubles as a kid. The fights, the teasing and the issues with the school. The thing with bullies is they generally don't stop. You have to be stronger than them, if not physically, then mentally. Sometimes there is only one option, to hold out. These people will get what is coming to them. They will get what they deserve at some point and he will be fine in the long run. It is tough for a kid to hear, but sometimes there are no other alternatives. I hoped he could handle it.

My visit with Toshi left me drained and I was happy to be hanging out back at home. It had been an exhausting week and I ended up back in the same headspace I had been spending my entire week in. I kept trying to think of some pre-emptive move. Something I could do to prevent anything from happening. I was at a loss. I guess I was waiting for things to escalate, although I didn't know how.

It left me uneasy but I had to soldier on. Business as usual. The next day I picked up my pound of Red Leaf. It was there as always. I left the cash for Jam and thought nothing of it. I distributed the portions to the proper parties and collected my money. Meanwhile, I was the mild-mannered plumber working like a regular guy. A girlfriend at home and everything was ordinary to anyone outside looking in. As time went on, it was like nothing ever happened. Three weeks later and I began to forget about the situation entirely. I had not heard or seen a thing. The paranoia faded away and I actually returned to business as usual, instead of just pretending.

My mustache was growing in thicker and thicker. G and I were raising twice the money for Movember as we did the year prior. I think people wanted to keep their goodwill with their drug dealer. My time with Aida returned to its natural state too. She finally stopped questioning me if 'something was up'.

At my real job, it was the same old routine. I had finished work on the Wednesday night prior to the holiday long weekend. I got to Aida's house and she wasn't home. I sat down on the couch and watched TV. I watched sports highlights until they repeated themselves, and still no sign of her. She was supposed to be home and I wondered what was keeping her. I was not one to be checking up on her. I simply wondered where she was. It wasn't characteristic of her to be late without a phone call or a text. I grabbed my phone and decided to call her. As it rang in my ear, I heard her ringtone. It was coming from the bedroom. I walked in and searched the room but didn't see her phone. I got down on all fours and looked under the bed to the source of the noise. A bright light from the phone was illuminating the dust collecting under the bed. This was weird. I grabbed the phone and hung mine up. I was staring at it while on my knees beside the bed. I couldn't comprehend what it could mean.

The bed in front of me was made perfectly normal except for a piece of paper on the pillow. She had left me a note. Of course she had left me a note.

"Yo. I kidnapped your girlfriend while you were running around. Don't be a hero. Do what is right and just give up the Red Leaf. She will be safe. Don't do anything stupid. Don't involve the cops. Just deliver what I want. I'll be in touch."

My eyes went wide and the paper in my hands shook. I don't know if it was fear, anger or helplessness. My body was not reacting in a way I deemed appropriate. I tried to convince myself I was dreaming. This kind of shit doesn't happen in real life, does it? It had to be a joke. Maybe G thought this was funny. When I tried to think of Aida in the hands of that guy, it made me sick. I considered vomiting right there on my knees beside the bed. I swallowed the urge, trying to focus my thoughts.

I stayed there on my knees by the bed for another minute running it through my head. Then I let out the loudest F-bomb I have ever dropped. I saw red. I was screaming and pulling at my hair. I got up and ran around the apartment. I picked up my phone, ready to place a call but I did not know to whom. Do I call the police? What if they weren't kidding? Do I call Jam? Shit, I didn't have his number so it didn't matter. It took a lot of restraint not to punch several holes in the wall. The only thing stopping me was not wanting Aida upset about it when I got her back home.

I was going to do anything to get her back. I couldn't think. I am not a religious man, but I found myself trying to talk to God. I was back down on my knees, the note still in my hand, looking up to the heavens and begging him to undo what had happened. I had reached a low point, and it turns out, even I could turn to God.

I fell to the ground, lying down in the fetal position, when I burst into tears. I cried. I bawled my eyes out like the day I lost my father when I was ten. I lost bodily control and convulsed on the ground, taking giant sobs and struggling to inhale.

This wasn't going to help her either. I needed to pull myself together if I wanted her back. I had to do something, and there was only one man I could talk to. He was not going to be happy to see me.

Baillargeon

Chapter 24

I didn't know what else to do.

I went to Jam's house. Following the same routine as last time, I doubled back several times. I was careful not to get followed. When I got there, I could sense something was not right. The once beautiful plants on his front step were withering away. That did not seem like him. I hopped up the three stairs to the door and the familiar lion's face was missing. I put my hands on the splintered remains left behind. Someone had torn it off the door. I knocked. No answer. I waited a while longer and wrapped again. Nothing. I grabbed the knob and turned. It was unlocked.

I pushed the door open and entered the house. I instantly got sick. It was like my internal organs had been torn from my insides. It was empty. Both my stomach and the house. I ran up the flight of stairs and peered into the farm. Nothing. The irrigation hoses and wiring for the lights hung from the roof. Any trace of the marijuana plants or the man who grew them were gone. On one of the irrigation hoses hung a piece of paper. I snagged it off the line and read it. I couldn't help but hear his Jamaican accent in my head while I read.

"Ey mon, I'm sorry for aving to do dis. I did not foresee sometin like dis appenin. I know I am leavin you in a tough situation, but I cannot get involved in dis type of ting. I wish you all dee best. Good luck.

"P.S. Take deese contents. Dey will elp you along your way."

Taped to the back of the note was a green Ziploc bag. Inside, mushrooms. I was furious. The man had screwed me. I swore if they hurt Aida I would track him down and beat him senseless. If he thought he could make amends by leaving me some of his super expensive mushrooms, he could go fuck himself. Jam was the only leverage I had. I wondered if I should search the house, maybe find a clue about where he went. This is why he needed the separation from me. If things went south, he was ready to bail. This was a plan B he had established a long time ago. I felt used. He had intrigued me and brought me close and I dove right in. I was fucked. He fucked me.

I stuffed the mushrooms into my pocket and made my way out of the house. I walked to the subway to head back into the city. My anxiety climbed higher every moment. It was probably because of the six fucking dudes who were watching me. They were not exactly subtle. It's hard to miss six giant muscle heads strutting down the sidewalk, each of them with the same stupid haircut. These were probably the ninja turtles I met the other night dressed in their other costume. Meat heads. They must have found two new members in the protein isle of a supplements store.

My ability to not have someone follow me had failed. I was obviously not paying as much attention as I thought to miss these fuckers in the first place. Another failure on a growing list. I went down into the subway and they followed. I went to the far end of the platform and awaited my train. They stood at the bottom of the steps acting nonchalantly as if they were not following and watching me. All while blatantly watching me. My train arrived and I waited until the last possible moment to squeeze through the doors. They had been standing near the edge of the platform. I hoped they never made the train.

I continued my ride staring out the window as nothingness flew by. Blackness, with the occasional flash of light, streamed past. I was getting back into the city and was several stops from home. I carried on looking out the window, trying to hide my face from anyone on the train. In the reflection, I saw someone sit next to me.

I turned to see Leonardo staring me down and five additional assholes standing over top of me. We were approaching a stop when Leonardo asked me to join him on the next platform. I got up and exited the train with them. There would be more options on a wide open platform than stuck in a train car. People cleared the platform with few stragglers waiting for the next train. I didn't see any help I could count on when we began talking at the far end of the platform. We were a long way from the stairs.

"Hello there, friend," Leonardo said to me. I was maintaining composure at the moment. It would be brief, as I could feel my face going red.

"Where the fuck is my girlfriend?" I tried to remain calm.

"Where have you been running around to today? Don't you have some pressing matters to attend to?" he ignored my question.

"Shut the fuck up and tell me where she is," my voice got stern. My hands turned into fists.

"Tell you what, take us to your dealer and your girlfriend will return home," he demanded.

Little did he know the grower had skipped town and I knew almost nothing about the man. He was a lost cause. Gone forever. They would never believe it, whether or not it was true. Letting him know could potentially have gotten me in more trouble. Leaving him to believe I could still deliver Jam was keeping Aida and me safe at the moment. None of this helped the fact that my blood was now boiling. My fists became tighter and my knuckles were turning white as old feelings ran through my body.

"How about I kick your fucking teeth in? Right after I finish knocking out each of your fucking lackeys. That's my counter offer."

"Even if you thought you could, how would that possibly help Aida? You have one bargaining chip here. It's Red Leaf. Don't be stupid."

Sadly, he was right. Just because I had Red Leaf, doesn't mean they couldn't hurt Aida and still dangle her life over my head. I didn't want a toe in the mail or something crazy like you see in the movies. I needed time to think. My option was down to the same result of these assholes threatening me last time. Run.

The stairs were behind a giant wall of Italian meat. Plus I had already decided not to antagonize them by going through them. I had one option they didn't expect. I hopped down onto the tracks and ran.

I took off as fast as I could, leaving screams from Leonardo behind me. Four of them jumped down onto the tracks and attempted to follow. They were obviously just free weight juice monkeys because their cardio was atrocious. This time I wasn't full of alcohol and I lost them immediately.

I was jogging down the tracks when the vibrations began. This clued me into a problem I had not put enough thought into. Getting hit by a subway was not one of the ways I wanted to go. I searched for a way out, just in case I couldn't make it to the next platform. The goombas might have been trying to get there from the surface themselves too. I found a giant metal door in the tunnel and decided to take it. City workers must assume people aren't dumb enough to walk down there, as I was surprised to find the door unlocked.

Now I was walking through absolute darkness. I had no idea where I was, or where I was going. I kept following the tunnel, wondering if I was walking towards or away from any potential exits. The only light I had was my cell phone, whose battery was dangerously low. The glow of the screen bounced off the smooth, solid cement walls of the corridors. I took my time as I searched for any signs of light or exits. I was alone. I was lost. Despair struck and I couldn't keep my composure. I found myself sitting on the floor, in the complete dark, and crying my eyes out. I had never experienced worse emotions in my life. Comparable only to losing my father. I don't know how long I was there for. It could have been several hours. I had to keep moving. I hit my cell phone for some light. Nothing. It was dead. I was completely consumed by blackness.

I made my way through the tunnel cautiously, feeling my way through. A few twists and turns and I found myself in the sewer. Not exactly what I was going for. As I walked through the stench and heat, my hand remained on the wall to guide myself through the tunnels. It was so dark, my biggest fear was tripping, falling and getting more than just my feet wet. I wandered for another hour, possibly two. It was difficult to keep moving. I was tired and worn out. I almost wanted to lie down and give up. The only thing motivating me were thoughts of Aida.

At one point I slowed to take a break. I leaned against the wall and I felt it give. The bricks moved. I pushed as hard as I could and several bricks fell in behind the wall. I kept working to push over the rest of them and a door took form. Behind it, there was a ladder to surface that was covered in vines, dimly lit from the moonlight above. It must have been unused for some time now and they bricked up this particular entrance. There had to be some reason for them to block this exit. It didn't matter because I wanted out of the stink filled sewer. I could keep venturing on through the dark of the tunnels hoping for the best, or take what could be a shortcut out of there.

I climbed up the ladder through the thicket of vines growing around it. Kicking my feet in and digging to grab the rungs, I made my way towards the moonlight streaming through a grate at surface. Using my back, I pushed up the heavy grate keeping me from escaping the tunnels. With maximum effort, I squeezed through the space, catching only my foot and losing at least three layers of skin on my ankle. I looked around and saw myself surrounded by chain link fence. It was like I was in some sort of cage. Searching the place, I located a door. It had a lock on the outside. Luckily I always carry a small tool (habit of the trade) and it happened to have a utility knife. It took some aggressive digging, with my hands barely fitting through the cage, but I pried open the lock to free myself. I could finally breathe fresh unrestricted air.

I was walking out of the complex when I had a realization of where I was. There were plenty of trees towering the area. There was only one place in the city like this. With that many trees with a number of facilities and fencing, I realized I was in Central Park. The zoo. At this point I worried about security. Also, because it was the middle of the night and in the park, I feared for almost everything else. I bolted as fast as I could in hopes nobody would notice I was there.

As I made my way back home I reflected on what had happened in the last few weeks. I had been threatened on numerous occasions, had to evade those goons twice, and my girlfriend was missing. Those pricks were responsible. It was time to go on the offensive.

Chapter 25-1

I went to Aida's and regrouped. It was five in the morning when I finally walked into the apartment. I had been walking for hours. Intertwined with emotional outbursts, my body begged for rest. I needed to lie down on the couch to gather my thoughts. I closed my eyes for a minute to process the information hounding me. Embarrassingly, I fell asleep. All the shit going on, and I took a nap. Characters in movies and TV shows always vow not to rest until they get someone back, but being that angry and confused is exhausting. It just kind of happened. I awoke several hours later and jumped off the couch.

I panicked, thinking I should be accomplishing something, but was not sure what. I thought I should at least get some one on one time with the guys in this organization. I decided I could start by chasing down the weed. I assumed G's buddy, our original supplier, was somehow connected. When the ginger knew so much about us and what we were doing, he had to have heard it through him. G had told me he was timid, a shy guy. I could most likely count on him for some information. It was time he and I finally met.

I knew where he lived. I had required that information from G in the first place. I wanted to know where to find him in case anything had ever went sideways. This wasn't a scenario I had imagined. Not knowing how to proceed, I walked up to his place and I introduced myself at the door. I don't think he had a clue what was going on. There was no way he would be that excited to meet me. His excitement also communicated to me that G told him more about me than he was ever supposed to. He invited me in and I wasted no time telling him the whole story of why I was there.

"What the fuck man? I hope you know I have nothing to do with this. I didn't know I was getting it from that guy. I just get it from some punk a friend had introduced me to. I thought I would just get a pound for myself to share with my friends, and G and I were talking about it, so I told him I would get an extra pound to share with him. I never asked my guy where he got it from. Thought I was better off not knowing, you know?"

The guy seemed upset. He was not a drug dealer. He lived in a nice apartment and looked like a decent human. Down to earth. He was a buddy of G's and got caught up. That didn't mean he didn't involuntarily fuck things up. I still had questions for him.

"Is that why you told him about Red Leaf? Where it was coming from?"

"Well I mentioned it to my guy. It was amazing stuff. G had brought me over a small amount, thought maybe I could sell some for him, but it was a small bag. I thought I could make some money if maybe my guy could get his hands on some. He told me he would eventually, but I wasn't allowed to take it from G. Otherwise I could be cut off. I didn't mean any harm by it."

"Nobody ever fucking does." I responded. "I am going to need to talk to your guy. Where can I find him?"

"There is a stash house he uses. Not far from here. It's a small apartment in Harlem. The windows are blacked out with garbage bags. It's a sketchy place. The guy is a punk. I would be surprised if he knew anything. His name is Larry. You will recognize him as he has a mohawk thing going."

I stood up to leave. There was no reason not to trust this guy. As I was walking out he called after me.

"I'm really sorry man. Tell G I really am."

I had stopped, turned around and was staring at him. Maybe I should have enlisted his help. Instead, I nodded at him and shut the door behind me.

I was making my way to the dealer's place when I noticed a crowd gathering ahead of me. They were staring up at the scaffolding on a building being renovated. I was on a mission and tried not to pay too much attention. However, the crowd was growing and there was something odd about the situation. There was a lot of banging and shaking of the scaffolding and I swear I could hear monkey noises. The city can be weird so I didn't concern myself and continued to walk. Maybe they were filming a movie. That's when a five gallon pail fell from above and landed in front of me. I was already in a bad mood and could have beaten the shit out of whoever let this happen. It could have prevented me from finding my girlfriend had I gotten injured.

I looked up and lo and behold there was a fucking monkey loose in the city. He was swinging around the pipes of the scaffolding, jumping from one section to another. He was a quick son of a bitch. There was what appeared to be animal trainers on top of the building and down on the sidewalk below. They were attempting to trap the animal. They had no idea what to do. The crowd was kicking back and watching this whole ordeal. Almost all were laughing at the spectacle.

The monkey was going nuts as they closed in on him. He was throwing whatever he could find at anybody who was getting too close. This was a crazy scene to witness. I stood there in awe watching this monkey bouncing around. I overheard the conversation with what appeared to be the animal experts and a police officer that had arrived at the scene. The monkey was in a temporary holding cage at the Central Park Zoo and it escaped due to a defective locking mechanism on the gate. He had been on the run for about thirty minutes.

Fuck me. There was a good chance I was responsible for that debacle. I thought of trying to lend my assistance. I decided against it as I had important things to attend to. If this monkey had kidnapped my girlfriend I would have thrown his ass off the building. Right then I had to keep my priorities in check. How hard could it be to subdue a monkey anyway? At least the building was structurally sound and not on fire. They would figure it out. I left that mess behind and set out to do what I intended. Find a drug dealer.

The rest of my walk was uneventful as I marched through the streets of NYC. It was a bright and sunny Thanksgiving afternoon and the paths were busy with tourists. I turned off the busy thoroughfare and headed towards the apartment building I was hunting down. At the address given to me there were ten units in the place. I noted the one with garbage bags in the window. I rang every buzzer except that one. A few people called down asking who it was, but the door still buzzed and I was allowed entrance to the building. You could always count on one person to have no care for the security of their building.

I walked up the stairs and down the hall. The carpet stained with numerous mysterious fluids. It was gross and thinned my patience. I approached the door and again realized I didn't know what I was thinking. Maybe it was because of how bad it smelled in there, maybe it was how gross and moldy the door was. I didn't want to touch it by knocking, so I booted it down. It crumbled at my feet in the fucking shithole of a building.

There was one undernourished man inside, sitting at a table with a giant bag of green in front of him. He was splitting his bags up for distribution. He jumped up from the table and faced me. He was the punk I was looking for, mohawk and all. He was so scrawny. He attempted to compensate by trying to look tough, or at least what he thought tough looked like. His torn up black jeans were like capris, showing off his pasty white chicken legs. His black vest only accentuated how skinny he was. He had enough metal attached to his face to be mistaken for Hellraiser. I thought the weight would make him top heavy and cause him to tip over. Worse yet, he had giant spacers in each of his ears. I knew I would enjoy this.

"Where is my girlfriend?" I thought I would be direct to see if he knew anything. A light bulb definitely went on as he figured out who I was.

"Who are you and what do you want?" He tried to sound hard. The fear in his voice betrayed him. I stared at him before he continued talking unprovoked. "I am sorry man, but your girlfriend must be in a different stash house."

"So you know who I am then?"

"Listen man, I've just heard rumours. Everyone knows about this new Red Leaf stuff and everyone is talking about it. I had heard there were plans in the works to get to the supplier so we could get in on that shit. Yesterday I heard rumours they found the guy and he wasn't giving it up so they were going to hold his girlfriend hostage until he did. We would have this new Red Leaf in no time. Dude, I have nothing to do with it man. I am just a dealer. I couldn't fathom doing anything like this."

"What do you mean you couldn't fathom? Look at you, you are a tough guy." I was laying on the sarcasm thick. "You are a big drug dealer. You get up to nefarious business. You must be rolling in dough to live in a place like this." I began moving towards him and he was growing nervous.

"I don't live here man. I just rent it to do my business." This stopped me in my tracks.

"Are you fucking serious, why the hell would you want to come here?" I couldn't understand this. "You could catch an STD from taking a leak while standing up. The clap is probably strong enough to swim upstream. Why the hell would you come here?"

"Look, it doesn't fucking matter. Why are you here?"

"I came to find my girlfriend, so where do I find her?" I asked as I inched closer to the guy.

"I have no idea." His hands rose up with both palms out, attempting to slow me down.

"Well, where do I find him? You know who I am talking about and don't fucking lie to me. I will squeeze the life out of you if I have to."

"How should I know man? I swear. I don't know where to find him," he pleaded, "there are layers to prevent this kind of thing. I get mine from a guy, who gets theirs from a guy and so on. My guess is the boss has her."

"How do I get to him?" I was now standing directly in front of him. His hands had lowered down to his sides. He was well aware of what I could do to him.

"Seriously dude, how am I supposed to know? I am at, like, the bottom rung. I am a peon, I'm nothing." He was now shaking, and pleading with me.

"Well who do you get your weed from? How many layers are there?" At this point I had both my index fingers wrapped through his spacers in his ears. I was gently pulling at both of them as his ears were gradually pulling away from his face.

He told me everything I needed to know without flinching. I had the name, description and address of the dealer he bought from. From what he had heard, there were eight layers, at least seven dealers above him. Guys weren't supposed to ever know more than one layer above. It kept the distance to the top. While I was at it, I asked him why he came to this shithole apartment, it was bugging me. The fucker lived with his parents. He was a privileged bastard pretending to be a bad ass. He attended private school. He was damn near crying after he spilled the beans to me. I let him know if he had been lying, I would be back to rip his ears right off his head. His parents would question the new look.

The cops are at an unfair disadvantage when trying to crack down on drugs. It is not like it's hard to find drugs. That is where you need to start. Find some drugs and climb the ladder. Everybody has a boss. They just have nothing to bargain with when dealing with these guys in the confines of the law. However, when faced with either telling you who they work for or strangling the life out of them, they always talk. Sometimes it's almost impressive how fast you can get them to spill it. This was one of those times.

Baillargeon

Chapter 25-2

The kid had given me enough to find the guy who would bring me one step closer to the man I was looking for. This guy was supposed to be so fat it would be impossible to miss him. He made it sound like I was looking for a sumo wrestler, except he was black. That was a weird thought. I wondered if there had there ever been a black sumo wrestler. I eventually looked it up. Emanuel Yarbrough.

I was walking to the address which wasn't far away. I could see my breath exhaling from my mouth. It was getting cold and winter was coming. It had been a long fall and the weather had been nice until now. My mustache was starting to capture the moisture of my breath. Stupid mustache. Even with how much I hated it, I wouldn't remove it until Aida gave me permission. I would do whatever she wanted. I had promised her I would keep it.

When I arrived at the house I could tell it was full of people. This guy was hosting Thanksgiving dinner. There was no way I was going to be able to go in with that many people there. I wanted to walk right in and get some answers, but a cooler head prevailed. I had to wait it out. It was chilly outside and there wasn't a point in waiting at the house. I left to find a nearby diner. Thanksgiving dinner alone in some shitty hole in the wall. Time hardly moved as I tried to occupy myself with the paper, which I read three times over. I waited till eight o'clock when I figured people may be moving on from the festivities. They would retire home to suffer in silence from over indulging.

Approaching the house, I was happy to see it was much quieter. Then I caught a lucky break. It was about time something worked out for me. At that moment, a man walked out of the house. There was no question who the man walking out of it was. The kid's portrayal to the man's girth was incredibly accurate. He was coming my way. He wasn't walking towards me so much as waddling. It must have been difficult to maneuver such a mass. It moved one side at a time. It was almost a runway model walk, all hips, except it was the furthest thing from sexy. It reminded me of the girl who turned into the blueberry at the Wonka Factory. This guy must have eaten a forbidden dark chocolate snack. He came waddling towards me, unaware of who I was. Otherwise he wouldn't have walked calmly into the shit storm I was about to bring down on him.

"Morton," I called out to him.

"Do I know you?" His bald head was sheen with perspiration from the thirty second stroll he had taken. With the temperature as low as it was, he was still sweating profusely. If it wasn't for the layers of fat insulating him, he was a high candidate for hypothermia.

I began to ramble, waiting for it to click with the big man.

"Maybe. Maybe not. I am sure you have heard of a guy at this point. The odd rumor about some guy and something called Red Leaf. Maybe how this guy has a girl, and this girl has gone missing. You might not know the man, but does this story sound familiar? Hell, maybe the man knows you."

"Listen man, I don't know what you are talking about," he said as he turned to walk away, back towards his house. I called out after him.

"Seems weird you're going back home then Morton. Seems to me like you were headed this way ten seconds ago."

I looked around the street. Not a lot of pedestrian traffic. If shit turned ugly the odd bystander may stick around. Generally you can trust a lot of New Yorkers to turn a blind eye. Even if it happened right there in the streets.

I followed him down the sidewalk. I could see him attempt to speed up. Faster and faster until his entire body was moving like a waterbed. He busted into his version of a sprint and I busted out laughing.

"Really? You are going to run from me? Where do you think you're fucking going?"

I caught up to him in a few simple strides and passed him. I turned around and he was still waddling along. I back pedalled in front of him. I kept chatting with him as I walked backwards in front of the big man.

"Listen to me Morton. Most of the time people in these situations say things like, don't worry, I am not going to hurt you." I was still back peddling as he was dripping sweat and breathing alarmingly heavy.

"Stop dumbass. Listen. I am going to fucking hurt you, that is, if you don't have a goddamned heart attack first. Where do you think you are fucking going anyway?" I was at a loss for words. This fat fuck couldn't produce any words either, whether or not he wanted to. He was going to keel over and die. He finally stopped. He bent over hyperventilating, trying to catch his breath. I walked up close to him and put my hand on his shoulder. I was about to comfort him. I felt so bad for him. Then he showed a surprisingly quick side, maneuvering up to stand and wrap his arms around me. I found myself in a tight bear hug.

I was not expecting that.

This man was obese and slow as fuck. I don't know how he managed to grab me. When he did, I found out he was strong. He was squeezing so hard I couldn't muster a scream of shock, let alone a breath. The real concern passing through my mind was that if he fell forward, it would kill me. He probably thought of this too. He would have had a tough time explaining to the police why he was lying on top of me when they showed up though. He would have been unable to stand himself back up.

When he had lunged for me I had been able to keep the arm I had on his shoulder free. The other stayed trapped between his arm and my body. It was currently crushed into my rib cage. He was grunting and breathing heavy as he attempted to squeeze the life out of me. I couldn't breath. Luckily my rib cage was holding out, protecting my internal organs. That meant I had enough time to react. As I ran out of air I could feel the pressure building up in my body. My eyes wanted to pop out of my head.

My fight or flight reflex was telling me to thrash about. That would have only served to exhaust me and allow air to escape from my system. I had one free arm and I had to decide how to use it best. I focused and thought about my next move. I took my free hand and brought it back as far as I could. I cupped my hand and swung it down hard over his ear.

He dropped me to the ground and began screaming in agony. He would not hear from that ear for some time. There was potential for it to be permanent, depending on the internal damage. Keeping a tight seal with the cupped hand when I struck, I had pressured up his inner ear and most likely ruptured his ear drum. Hurts like hell. I didn't get my hearing back for three weeks after I had it done to me once.

"Sorry about that Morton. You didn't leave me much choice."

"Mmmuuup……..Mmmup," he was making sounds to test his hearing. He was down on one knee with his finger in his ear, wiggling it around in there while his face grimaced.

"I wouldn't do that if I were you. It's going to be like a mosquito bite. It will be nice to scratch, but it will only make things worse. If fluid starts coming out it will be time for a doctor." I was here to get information from him and I had no problem using violence. What I didn't know was how much he deserved going deaf at this point. I almost felt bad. Maybe it was because I had experienced that pain before. I had sympathy.

"Listen to me. No more funny business. I came here to find out what or who you know. I know you get your dope from him, if only indirectly, so you tell me how to find him. Or at least tell me who knows how to find him. You don't want to go deaf in both ears over this. If you take it far enough you will end up blind too."

I figured that threat should do the trick.

From there it was too easy. He put up some resistance. The usual stuff about not knowing shit or how much trouble he could get in for talking. They could kick the shit out of him or kill him. In the end, he knew there was no way out for him. He was lucky too, because torturing him was not going to be difficult and may have been comical. I had so many options. I could have starved him and then left a pile of McDonald's just out of reach. He would have sold out his mother for a Big Mac within an hour.

The big man stayed down on one knee for the remainder of the interrogation. He was in discomfort with his ear. I moved to the other side of his body so he could better hear me. I remained far enough away that he wouldn't try anything funny again. Shame on me if I were to get caught up with him twice.

I asked him a bunch of questions to which he had few answers for. The chubby man wasn't a big bad guy. He was in the middle of hosting dinner and he still had family at his house. He was only running out for ice at the moment. He wasn't trying to be some gangster. He actually told me he wasn't a drug dealer. He called himself an intermediary between friends. I felt terrible unexpectedly for his ear. He rationalized his dealings the same way I had.

Since he didn't know much he only told me where he goes to buy. It was a woman. I asked if I should be concerned about her. He could see how she could be a feisty one. I apologized to him for the ear again, and hoped everything would be alright. I wasn't too sorry though. I still stole his cell phone before parting ways. My battery had died with my running around and he had this girl's number in his phone. I was going to need it.

I was climbing the ladder. The second dealer. Possibly another six. This was going to take a while. Unfortunately for them, my resolve was high. I headed away from Morton's place. It was perfect timing as I could see fireworks over the horizon. It was Thanksgiving evening and someone was illegally setting them off in a park or their backyard. They lit up the darkening sky.

I looked at them and thought of the celebration. It was a time for family. I missed Aida. I wasn't going to slow down now.

Chapter 25-3

It was getting late. Coming up on midnight. I figured the woman could be out at this hour on a holiday weekend. There was no harm in checking her place out. What else was I going to do mid-rampage?

I made my way to her shitty apartment in Chinatown. The whole neighborhood reeked from the day's activities. At this time of night, the lights still lit up the main roads. It was a ghost town in the alleys that were typically packed with people and their shitty wares during the day. A couple blocks off the main road and it got darker and ominous. I walked up to the place and looked to the apartment window I believed to be hers. There were no lights on. I thought I could try simply ringing the buzzer. No answer. It could have been a long night if I had to sit there waiting for her to come home. I had one other shot.

I had taken Morton's cell phone, so I figured I may as well use it. Her name was in the address book. I gave it a call. She answered. I had no idea what I was going to say. Calling may have been a bad idea. It was loud in the background, and while I knew she was speaking, I couldn't hear a word she said. It sounded like she was in a night club listening to some God-awful house music. I hung up as it wasn't going anywhere. The phone call was bad idea anyway. I sent her a text instead.

Me: Where are you?

Her: what the fuck u want??

Me: I'm in need. Needs done tonight. Got a good thing going. Can you help me out?

I needed to be as vague as possible. At this point she would have no reason to believe she wasn't talking to Morton. If I used language Morton would never use or tipped her off in any way it could have been dangerous. I waited for a response.

Her: u r not supposed to text me u fat fuck. be at my place in 15. gotta make this quick.

I hid in the shadows for the next fifteen minutes. As a normal human being, I feared someone jumping out from a dark corner when I was out. You are nervous anyone could be waiting for you. It is odd when you become that guy in the corner. Turns out being that guy hiding and waiting is nervous too. My adrenaline was pumping as I sat in the shadows and waited.

A few people came walking by during those fifteen minutes. I was nervous as I couldn't tell which one was going to be her. When she did come by, I knew right away. She had been at a club and dressed appropriately. With a red and white dress and a big bow in her hair that had a ribbon running down her backside, this girl was ready to party. She made a move to the front door of her building which confirmed it. I stepped out from the shadow.

She jumped and clutched at her chest when I called out her name. After the initial shock I caught her making glances to her keys that were still hanging in the lock of her door. Her eyes were wide and she held her arms crossed as if to protect her body from me in fear. I totally understood. I was a strange man that just ambushed her at her front door. I could tell she was ready to run. I tried to alleviate her fears.

"Don't worry," I said, trying to calm her, "Morton sent me. I just need to chat with you."

"What did that fat fuck get me into?" she asked.

I stepped towards her. Now that I was close enough to prevent her getting inside, I said "Morton may not be around too much anymore. Not near you at least. I came here for answers, not a hookup. I need to meet your boss." I grabbed her arm and brought her in closer to me.

I had told myself to keep my guard up. I had made the mistake with Morton already. I had learned nothing. Shame on me. I didn't expect this chick to have it in her so I wasn't prepared for it when she kneed me square in the nuts. I let out a deep groan and folded over. She shook her arm free and backed away, trying to catch my next move. I attempted to straighten up, only to be reminded how much a shot in the nuts hurts. I went down on one knee and struggled to stay upright as I braced myself on the pavement with my free hand. The initial pain is from shock, followed by a brief moment where you think you will be fine. That is when the pain goes from the balls and travels up to the stomach making you believe you may throw up. I swear I could have lost my minimal stomach contents had I let it go. Then it continues to move up the body and gets stuck in your throat. You inexplicably start coughing. Finally, it hits your eyes. They are shut tight and when you open them, a single tear falls from your bloodshot and watered sockets. I watched through my teary eyes. She turned and ran away from me. She wasn't moving too fast in her heels.

My testicles had migrated to my throat and I swallowed to get them back down to where they belonged. I controlled the urge to vomit. I ignored the tears streaking down my cheeks and did my best to limp after the bitch. When I finally caught her, I tackled her to the ground. I was still reeling from the shot to the nads, so I did nothing but hold on to her while she flailed about. I was breathing deep, trying to compose myself.

I got back to my feet once I had regained some self-control, holding on to her as I straightened up. She was still squirming as I was still trying to get my wits about me. I shook her to get her attention and let her know she wasn't going anywhere. When she finally stopped moving I had an urge to slap her across the face. I had never hit a woman before, but my boys wanted vengeance. I maintained my thirty year streak of not striking a woman. I realized I had sprung up on her and she reacted as any reasonable woman would have. I should have expected that sort of response.

She attempted a new strategy and let out a large scream while trying to writhe out of my grasp. I scolded her. "Shut up! Go sit down and don't do anything stupid." I pointed at a bus bench. I scanned the streets and didn't see anyone watching. No lights flickered on with her outcry. Probably a common occurrence around there. She sat on the bench while rubbing her arm as if I hurt her. I was mad because I feel like I got the worst of the exchange.

I had already wasted too much time and energy on this woman. I quickly explained my situation as I had to her cohorts before her. I concluded with telling her I needed to find her boss.

"I can't tell you. He will kill me."

I was getting real fucking tired of hearing that. People watch too many movies. The only real threat is the one in front of you.

"He will be lucky to be around when I get a hold of him. I wouldn't worry about him."

My patience was thin and I wasn't giving much thought to my answers.

"And if you fail, what will I do? The guy is fucking crazy."

"You probably have money. I am not robbing you. Go back to China or some shit." I answered.

"I'm from Korea you fucking asshole."

"Oh, me so solly," I responded with a terrible accent and my hands pressed together as I bowed to her. I knew it was unnecessarily racist. My temper was short and my balls were killing me. I got nice and angry as I yelled at her, "I don't give a shit what you do. All I know, is I will literally fucking kill you this fucking minute if you don't tell me what I want to hear."

I think this snapped her out of her confusion and self-pity. The flood gates opened and she spilled everything. It was like the gears in her head had completely shifted.

"I'll tell you who I get my shit from. He is a skin headed Aryan Nation prick. If you were to kill him you would be doing this world a favor. He treats me like shit every time I see him. This is who they put me in touch with."

You could see her frustration had been building for some time. I was the catalyst that was unleashing her thoughts. Maybe she saw this as a way out.

"I've tried to switch dealers but I think they get a kick out of this guy. He is a total whacko. I don't know why I considered protecting him. I guess I am just afraid for myself. If you don't get him to talk, you have to kill him or run him out of town. Otherwise I am as good as dead."

"Don't worry. I will take care of every asshole standing in my way."

"The guy is tough not to notice. Anyone with a swastika neck tattoo usually stands out in a crowd. He is a skinny white bitch with a shaved head. They use him for their dirty work. He keeps the street people in line. He is not afraid to get his hands dirty. He especially likes fucking with the colored folk. Fucking prick."

Her hatred of this guy was oozing through now. She wasn't going to hold back at this point. We kept talking and she gave me the details I needed.

"If you hate him so much, why do you deal with him?" People like her confused me.

"I need money, and he is the only guy they will let me buy from."

Her answers were simple and made sense to her. They were idiotic to me.

"Maybe you shouldn't be selling dope. Why do you?"

"Shit man, I am just trying to make it, I need money. I can't afford to complain. I got family still in Korea trying to get over here. Do you have any idea how costly that is?"

"Well then get a real job, or at least a new supplier. This one is going out of business. Make better decisions," I told her, talking down to her. I was growing tired of excuses.

"Says the guy who let his girlfriend get kidnapped. Worry about your own shit."

That hurt to hear. My motivations were not the best either and definitely caused me issues. I was already learning my lesson the hard way and I didn't need to hear that shit. Not from her.

"Watch your mouth. You don't know anything about me."

"Fuck you. You probably have a cunt of a girlfriend and you deserve this. I hope she is getting raped and beaten for the shit you've caused." It was like she switched gears again. Maybe she was bipolar.

"Cut that shit out right now," I yelled at her as I stood up from the bench. She was getting more aggressive. Maybe she sensed that I didn't have it in me to be violent with a woman. She stood up, getting in my face and becoming confrontational.

"You fucking pussy. I don't know why I have told you shit. You think you are so fucking tough. You are probably going to get killed for this. When you do, I am going to find your grave and take a piss on it." Things had turned quickly. I couldn't understand it. I already had what I wanted. I gave her a look that equated to 'whatever' and turned to walk away.

She grabbed me, spun me around and dove in for a kiss. Right on the lips. I went to push her away but at that moment she grabbed onto my cock. Not in a nice way. She may have thought I would enjoy that, but I was far from pleased.

I slapped her across the face. I didn't feel great about it. I didn't feel bad either. A thirty year streak ended. At least my balls were freed and avenged. They rejoiced.

She sat back down on the bench, rubbing her check looking incredulous.

"Are you embarrassed? You look like your blushing." I joked about her cheek turning bright red from the impact of my hand.

"Fuck you," she retorted. She didn't find me funny. This made me laugh. This bitch was insane and I had no empathy for her.

I didn't have time to deal with the broad so I left her there on the park bench, holding her cheek. It was on to the next dealer. I was going to have to surprise this guy in the middle of the night. It was well past midnight. Black Friday.

Baillargeon

Chapter 25-4

I grabbed a cab and gave the driver an address to the next stash house. The fourth dealer. At that pace things were going to catch up to me. I had been squeezed into a near coma, kneed in the balls so hard I was still struggling to swallow and now I was going to some skin head's lair. Shit was getting progressively worse. I leaned my head against the window as I watched the city go by. The buildings and streets got darker and sketchier as we drove.

The cab driver dropped me off and peeled out of the neighborhood. It was not pretty. This piece of garbage lived in an apartment building that looked like it housed some of the lowest people in the city. You would think these Aryan Nation mother fuckers would notice a correlation with what they do and how they live. I guess that is why they are so angry. Not to mention this building was in an ethnic neighborhood. Do they choose to live amongst those they hate, or is it why they become this way? Blame those around them instead of taking personal responsibility? It makes no sense for them to live there. It's like someone with a peanut allergy working in the Planters factory. I will never understand it.

I walked through the building's security door that was no longer providing much security. It was off its hinges and hung like the dilapidated screen door from the deep south. I closed it behind me with care. I was afraid it would fall off and wake the whole building.

I was at the point where my brain was not working as well as it should. I was tired. Not knowing how to approach the situation, I struggled to concoct a plan. I walked up a few flights to his door at the top of the stairs on the third floor. I was standing at this door, staring at it. I was at a loss. It was two in the morning. I tried to think, instead I knocked with conviction. Continuing to improvise.

I heard shuffling around. He was in there. I could hear the muffled curses as he moved about and came to the door. He opened it up and I saw this man for the first time. He had been sleeping and he answered the door in a pair of boxer shorts, exposing his numerous tattoos across his body. The majority of them were hate related. There was anger in his eyes as he narrowed them at me, furrowing the brow of his shaven head trying to figure out who I was. He stared at me, and with a scowl on his face, directed his yelling and cursing at me.

"Who the fuck are you and why the fuck are you knocking on my door at two in the fucking morning?"

I threw a quick punch right in his fucking face. I could already tell there was going to be no negotiating. Not with this fuck. I was going to have to beat it out of him. Needless to say I caught him by surprise. One minute he is sleeping, the next he is eating my fist. Tough night for him.

That must have woken him up. He was surely confused but now he was coming at me. He fought wildly, like a rabid dog. Although he had clearly done this before, he fought with pure strength, determination and ability to take a punch. He lacked discipline though. You have to fight with your head first.

He spent his time winding up for haymakers to try land one glorious punch to end it. These telegraphed so far in advance. A simple step to the side or keeping ones forearms up to block the attack was what it took to avoid any damage.

Short jabs were the more efficient form of attack in a street fight. I pulled my elbow back keeping my forearm straight and continued to throw them right at the soft bridge of his nose. I was aiming for blood as soon as possible. The adrenaline would overtake any pain from punches landed and would not slow him down. The sight of gushing blood from ones face would usually incite a response though. This guy only went wilder. He grabbed me by both shoulders and bull rushed me through the drywall. My back left an imprint of where we landed. If we had hit a stud, that would have hurt.

Both his hands were clutching at my shirt. He tried to jab at my face while not letting go. Although he was giving me a few shots to my chin and lower lip, these were of little threat. He would have to let go to do any damage and that was when I could strike. He pulled his right hand off to throw a punch and I used my now free left to grab at his bicep and push back. This opened his stance as his foot had to back up with the push to maintain balance. My knee came up and had a direct shot into his balls.

I have been in a lot of fights and have won the majority of them. One of the reasons was because I had no issues fighting dirty. The more they deserved it, the less I felt bad about it. He keeled over but didn't go down to the ground. He doubled over and turned his head up to me. I brought down my right hand onto the side of his face. This time he went down. I thought that might finish him. I underestimated how resilient this cock sucker was. He was attempting to get up and I didn't want to give him a second of recovery time. I took the three steps between us in a half run and tackled him back down to the ground. We wrestled for a short time. The few big shots he had taken left him in no shape to manage the fight. I got on top of him and unleashed a flurry of punches down on him. He squirmed and attempted to block them with his hands. When I finished raining down fists upon him, I leaned back and stood up over top of him.

He was a sorry looking sight. This guy was lying on his own living room floor at two in the morning, nose broken, missing at least one of his front teeth with another chipped, and his left eye was swelling up. All of that hurting, and he was still only cradling and massaging his balls. He was covered in both of our blood. My blood was dripping from my bloodied knuckles. It was probably the result of knocking out his teeth. I had to remember to disinfect my hands later. This guy was dirty.

He lay there, gasping for air and spitting blood out at the sides. I opened up to talk to him for the first time.

"I know you are hurting. Keep in mind I can still make things much worse. Tell me how I find the girl."

"Fuck you," he squeezed out. Relentless fuck.

I put my foot down on top of his groin and gradually put my weight on it. His pain became audible through loud groans.

"You may want to re-think your attitude."

"Okay, okay," he yelped.

I let off and took a step back. He got up and I didn't see any harm in it. I was confident he didn't have any fight left in him. He struggled to his feet. He was holding his insides and moaning every inch of the way. He stood up only to flop down onto the nearby couch. He was bleeding over his shitty furniture.

"So you're the guy hey? Red Leaf?" he asked me.

"Maybe I am. Maybe I'm a friend of his."

"Well friend, I may know some people. I could get you real close to your girlfriend. Or at least to the guy who knows exactly where she is. Why should I help you?"

"Because I have no qualms with wiping you off the face of this earth. I feel like it would be my duty as a human being to improve this world. Now I would rather not have to do that. I believe in miracles, you could maybe turn it around." I was trying to give him a glimmer of hope. I was not optimistic for his future.

"I'll tell you what. I know where you can find a guy who will know. He is a couple steps up the ladder, way up on the chain. Maybe I can give you him."

"How do you know him then? I thought there was separation between the layers."

"If I were to guess, they doubted I would blow the whistle on this guy. I don't take kindly to police officers or threats. I also don't take kindly to Jews and colored folk either. This guy is the right hand man. When they need shit taken care of in the streets he comes and talks to me directly. I take care of the streets. But this guy needs to go. He is a goddamn nigger. I am tired of taking orders from him. But what are you gonna do for me?"

"Don't be asking what I can do for you, and start asking what I could do to you. You feel that pain in your balls right now? I will make you feel ten times that pain. That will be before I fucking cut them off. How's that for a start? You aren't getting anywhere in that condition and I got all night."

"Alright, alright. You let me go and I'll give him to you. That guy shouldn't have that much money and power anyway. Thinking he can tell me what to do. Guys I need to take care of. He should be on the nigger duties. Meanwhile he is living the high life, pretending to be white. Makes me sick."

This guy was a real piece of work.

"Where do I find him?" I asked.

"At his house or his yacht. He has tons of money. The yacht season is over, so I imagine it's in the slip down at the harbour. He stores stuff there in the winter." He was laboring through the words. Spitting blood on his carpet between sentences.

He filled me in on information I didn't even ask for. All the while he was looking around, fidgeting on the couch. I figure he was testing how his body still worked. I was beginning to see he was plotting. He was dragging on his details and descriptions as if he was trying to drag this out for time.

"That is everything I need. For being a good sport about this, I promise I will keep you out of this. Nobody will know you gave them up. Does that work for you?" I wanted to be done with him and it was time to go. As I walked to the door he called out to me.

"Yeah, works for me. I wouldn't have told you anything if I thought I would let you leave here alive anyway." I was standing in the still open doorway. I turned back to see he had gotten up off the couch and was charging at me. He had a knife he must have had stashed in or around the couch. I was halfway out the door and standing at the top of the stairs. While he rushed at me my only thought was evasion. As he approached I was standing square to him as if prepared to fight him. He was running with such velocity to tackle me that when he lunged I merely side stepped him. A matador escaping the gouge of a bull's horn. He managed to clasp onto my arm with his free hand and pulled me with him as we both fell down the stairs. I was able to grab the railing at the top and my body spread out over the top four steps.

He was not so lucky. He rolled down the steps and collapsed at the bottom. He did not flinch. With the ruckus on the steps I knew someone would peak out of their apartment to see what the commotion was about. I backed into his room. Someone did come out and saw him on the landing. A Spanish lady in her nightgown came from the floor below and I watched as she turned him over. His own knife lodged into his chest during the fall. The woman screamed and looked around as I backed into the apartment unseen, the door still wide open. I checked out the kitchen window to find a different exit and was happy to see a fire escape. I climbed down as fast as I could and got the hell out of there. The cops would be there shortly.

As I made my way home I thought of what could link me to the place. Aside from some of my blood from our fight, and the evidence of the beating he took at my hands, there was nothing. With no reference to compare strange blood to and no possible connection for them to ever come looking for me, I was in the clear. I didn't kill him anyway. That was accidental suicide, and by God if he didn't deserve it.

Baillargeon

Chapter 25-7

That had been a close call. I needed to keep moving. If Aida was housed with someone like that, she was in danger and it was my job to protect her. I had little left in me and couldn't imagine having to deal with another Nazi. I would have to find the resolve as needed.

My improvisation worked pretty well, even if it ended with a dead skin head. I was getting closer, so I decided to keep it up. I had to take a train to the next house as it was nowhere near where I was. There were not a lot of cabs cruising that disgusting neighborhood looking for fares. It took several trains and a cab ride to get to the fancy neighborhood I was heading to. When I finally made it to his place, it was a fancy fucking house too. A mansion some may call it.

It was now four in the morning. I would have suspected to arrive at another quiet house like the last. This guy was still awake. The lights were on and I could hear music pounding inside. Techno. I thought he might be having a party. I couldn't hear any people and didn't see a whole lot of vehicles around. I was getting sick of this shit. It had worked once before, so I went ahead and rang the doorbell.

There may not have been a traditional party happening at the house, but this guy was partying. He opened the door, revealing a short, stocky, clean cut African American male. The man's eyes were wide with no color since his pupils were so dilated. No doubt he was coked right up. It explained the four in the morning solo dance party. Aside from that, he fit the part for his house. If this guy was a huge drug dealer he made himself up like any other Wall Street money man. I decided to take a different tactic than I did with the Nazi. I wasn't going to punch him in the face immediately.

"Can I help you?" he asked me, adjusting his cuffs on his suit as he must have thrown his jacket on when he heard the doorbell ring. Maybe he was expecting someone. He was pulling and tugging things straight as if to present himself to me. It appeared to be an expensive suit, but I was not the guy that could tell the difference. Let alone be impressed by it.

"I came to ask you a few questions, if you don't mind." I was sizing him up. He wasn't a big guy, kind of short. Put together and well groomed. I thought he would probably be afraid of taking a punch to the face. I was hoping that would work to my advantage.

"You a cop?" he asked.

"Nope, just some guy with some questions."

With only that, he waved me into his home. We entered into a large foyer. The classic rich persons' house with a large staircase wrapping around the room. There was one small table with flowers on it in the centre of the foyer. He walked in and let me soak it in. It was like he was trying to show off to me. I found his willingness to talk to some stranger odd. Once I was inside he shut the door and turned to me.

"What can I help you with?" he asked. The techno music was still blaring upstairs. He ignored its existence and focused his attention on me.

"Well," the words came out before I knew where the sentence was going. He looked like a regular enough guy. I thought I could be straight with him. "I'm the guy everyone has been talking about. The guy with Red Leaf," as I made quotation signs in the air around Red Leaf. "My girlfriend has gone missing and I need to find her. I want nothing to do with this and would like to take her home."

I thought I was being cordial, but the more I talked the more agitated he became.

"How did you come to find me?" he asked. A frown broke on his brow.

"One of your dealers. He told me where to find you. I just need you to tell me where to find my girlfriend." I was trying to become forceful to see if he would cave. He only became increasingly agitated.

"Who? Who told you?"

"It doesn't matter." I replied.

He was getting angry. "It does fucking matter. I will fucking kill him." He was now irate and losing his calm and collected demeanor. I had a feeling it was not the best time to tell him he was already dead. The situation was escalating. The tension was telling me I would have to resort to violence.

"Listen, all I want to know is where my girlfriend is. You tell me and I leave here without any trouble."

The guy laughed. A loud and boisterous laugh. I didn't know what he found so fucking funny. It came across as cocky and I was starting to realize he was not what he portrayed himself to be. Now I was getting irate. I decided that was enough talk. The laugh sealed it. I took a step towards him.

He kicked me. I literally didn't see it coming. It's not something bar brawlers get into. He kicked me right in the face before I flinched. I dropped to the ground and immediately crawled back on to my feet to reset. His eyes never left me while he removed his jacket, as if getting ready for dinner, and placed it over the stair railing. Somehow I underestimated another cock sucker. I must have been worn-out, because I was starting to have a poor track record with these assholes.

He turned to address me directly and got into a fighting stance, like someone in The Matrix or the octagon. It had one way to go now. I ran at him to tackle him to the floor which he defended like a professional. His legs went back as he braced himself by leaning into me and dropped sharp elbows onto my back. I tried to pull away but he put me in a head lock before I backed away. He tossed me aside, wrenching my neck further than I believe it is supposed to go.

I jumped back to my feet and got my hands up. He came towards me, slipped my hands, and landed a couple shots in my face. I backed off, trying to regain some semblance of control. I was leaking a fair amount of blood over my left eye already. I couldn't let it deter me. He came at me, thinking I was weak, and he threw a hook I managed to counter with a solid shot to his cheek bone. He staggered back. Thank God, he was human.

My celebration didn't last long as he threw a flurry of gut shots. My abs were not exactly developed for this type of punishment. I was going breathless. He then reached down and grabbed my left leg, lifted it in the air, and slammed his body into my chest. It took me down to the floor and removed any trace of wind I had left.

He maneuvered to sit on my chest and rained blows directly on to my face. I went limp after the third shot, and judging by the pain and bruising, I would say he may have struck me three more times. I must have blacked out. When I came to he was standing over me. He was asking me questions and rambling on as if I wasn't half dead on the floor.

"The only reason you are alive is because you have the best weed. My boss wants you alive. If it were up to me, you would be dead already. I guess there would be a concern someone else could start up with Red Leaf. Whatever, I'm not paid to think," he was rambling. I think he realized this and broke it up by kicking me in the ribs. Fuck me, it hurt.

"So just tell me where to find this weed. Stop making this difficult on yourself," he said as he leaned down and pulled my head closer to his by grabbing a handful of my hair. He pulled his other arm back for what was about to be a devastating blow to my face.

"It's one guy," I blurted out, "and he is gone. He took off when shit hit the fan. There is nothing I can do. I just want my girlfriend to be safe. She has nothing to do with this. Please." I had turned to begging. I had nothing left.

This guy had taught me a lesson in fighting in under thirty seconds. I had been surprised by a few of these guys, but I had underestimated them. For the first time, I realized how much trouble I was really in. These weren't bar fights anymore, these guys meant business. I was in over my head and terrified.

"You better go find him then. Do whatever it takes to track him down. I'll give you two days and you will come back and see me. If you don't come back, or come back without the information I want, I will personally cut your girlfriend's pretty throat." He continued to give me instructions. I continued to lie on the floor bleeding.

"I'll be watching you. Don't fuck about. If you try to run, if you try anything smart, next time I won't stop. I will end you, no matter how strong your pot is." He paused and walked over to the mantle where he picked up a jewelry box and brought it over.

"I want you to take a look at this." Inside was a collection of jewellery, watches, rings, and a shoelace. "This may not look like much, but you do not yet know what it means. This is a piece of every person that has screwed with me. They are gone now. Gone by my hand. If you fuck with me, I will rip that ugly fucking mustache right off your face and find a way to keep it in here. You understand me?"

He was confident I wouldn't screw him. Also confident I didn't pose any threat to him at this point either. I hadn't put up much of a fight. I tried to pull myself off the floor. My face was stuck as the blood was drying between my face and the tile. I peeled myself back and struggled to pull myself up. First, onto my hands and knees, where I had to stop and take a breath.

"That's it my man. Pull yourself together. I know you can do it," the cocky asshole joked.

I achieved verticality with maximum effort. Bringing myself to my feet, holding my rib cage as I was short of breath. I was staring out through a red tint as blood flowed into my eyes. The taste of iron was rampant throughout my mouth and I wanted to spit in the worst way. The guy might have killed me if I did. I wobbled my way to the door, staggering and grasping at the wall and tables as I went. He was chuckling behind me.

I wanted to stay. I wanted to continue trying to fight him. I wanted to beg for mercy, beg for my girlfriend. I was done. I contemplated turning around, telling him everything, start to finish, try to appeal to his decency. I knew nothing would help. I was going home. It was my only option. Maybe if I tried hard enough, I thought I could maybe find Jam. I opened the door.

"Don't forget man. I expect to see you soon. Don't let my boss down. However, if you do, you will be making me happy. This was fun. Let's do it again sometime."

I was out the door before he finished and began searching for a cab. When one finally pulled over, he didn't want to let me in. He was afraid of getting blood on the car. I tossed cash through the open window and pleaded for a bit of sympathy as I had just been hit by a truck.

"Why don't you get ambulance? They take care of you." He shouted in some thick foreign accent.

I merely said my address and told him I would be careful not to bleed on his fucking plastic seats.

It was an uncomfortable ride home. Some of that was because he kept checking me out in his mirror with disgust, but mostly because it felt like I had actually been hit by a fucking truck.

-      -   -   -   -   -   -

I went back to Aida's house and I hopped in the shower to clean myself up. The water was like acid burning my skin. It flowed off me red and pooled in the drain. As I climbed out of the shower I was afraid to towel off. I stood there naked, drip drying on the floor in front of the sink. My face was on fire, and I was scared to glance in the mirror. I took a deep breath and lifted my head. After an ocular assessment of the damage, I concluded I should be alright. I had no broken bones and most of my wounds would heal with band aids and time. I was still covered in a shit load of cuts and bruises. Worse yet was the terrible unnerving depression that I may have got my girlfriend and I killed. Oh, and hoping for no internal bleeding.

After I got cleaned up I fell onto our bed and immediately drifted to sleep. My body could not move on without it, regardless of what had been happening.

I had the craziest dream. I was gardening, which I have never done before, and I was picking turnips. I don't even like turnips. A big frog appeared out of nowhere and hopped towards me. It was like he meant to do me harm, so I took one of the turnips and whipped it at him as hard as I could. When it hit him, he exploded into bubbles, like soap bubbles or some shit, and floated away. Freud would impress me if he could analyze that shit. It was probably a concussion from a kick to the face. It was messing with my brain. It was uncomfortable to say the least. I woke up confused in a cold sweat.

Pain replaced confusion in a hurry as my body reminded me of what had happened. Everything hurt. I checked the clock and it was eleven in the morning. I had been out six hours and had wasted too much time. My worry for Aida compounded the soreness. I went through the house to find anything that could dull the hurt. I took the remaining four aspirin in the bottle, but I knew that would not cut it. No other painkillers at my disposal. Not even a bottle of booze. I could have called my brother. Tell him to bring help in the form of drugs. I was afraid he would react in an inappropriate way if he saw me. Best to keep him away from me.

I was on the couch, contemplating what my next move was. There was no way I was going to locate Jam. The man had shown me how clever he was. If he didn't want to be found, I was not going to find him. I had no Red Leaf and would never in a million years be able to figure out how he made it. I thought maybe if I told him whose it was, they could try track down Jam. Then they could let her go. I would tell them every piece of information I knew about him. The problem was, I did not know that much. I didn't know his real name for fuck sakes. He played this a lot better than I did. Maybe he knew this could happen. If I gave them what I had on Jam, I worried he still wouldn't let Aida and I go anyway. There was no way he would be that reasonable. I was fucked.

I broke down and cried again. I had cried more in those two days than all the times since I was twelve combined. I had no idea what I was going to do. As the tears ran down my cheek, the salty discharge ran into my wounds on my face and caused them to sting more. At that low point, I saw the green bag of mushrooms on the table. Jam had told me they would bring me new life. When I was down they would save me.

Getting high was not the answer. What I needed to do was think and that's not something I have ever done well while on mushrooms. I was convincing myself how bad of an idea it would be, all the way until I had finished the whole bag. If these were special mushrooms, they still tasted like regular ones. Shitty.

If there was one lesson I had ever learned in life, it was when your girlfriend had been kidnapped, your life was in shambles, and you may be facing an imminent death, you shouldn't do mushrooms. However, in this particular moment it seemed logical. At least it would get me through the next several hours physically. Maybe, just maybe, I was hoping come up with some fucked up idea I haven't thought of yet to solve my current dilemma.

Then it happened. About forty-five minutes later, they hit me. Hard. At first my body went numb, which made me ecstatic. My physical pain was gone. My emotional pain was still present. I was going to have to act quickly. I got up and darted around the apartment.

Then my phone rang. I checked the call ID. It was Toshi. Shit. He would want to discuss what we were planning on doing Sunday. I know this was not an appropriate time to talk on the phone with a child. A beat up drug dealer high on mushrooms was not the best role model. I had legitimate concerns it might be my last time talking to him. I picked up the phone.

"Hey Toshi. I am so sorry. I am going to have to cancel this Sunday. I have too much on the go and I'm so busy. I'm sorry bud."

"Oh, ok. I understand." He sounded dejected.

"I know bud, and hopefully I can make it up to you. I just have some things to take care of. Okay?"

"Okay. Is there anything I can help with?" He was so innocent. If only he could. I tried my best to explain it to him.

"No bud. Sorry, but you can't. Remember a couple weeks ago when you told me about your bullies? Well I have some bullies of my own that I am not sure how to take care of. They are stronger than me."

"Well," he said, "I know you said you have to be stronger than them, either physically or mentally. So maybe you can be stronger or smarter? You said they usually get what they deserve in the end. The question I only thought of later, was what if you were the thing that was supposed to give them what they deserved?"

"I hear you buddy. I'll see what I can do. I gotta run for now though, but you take care. I'll talk to you later okay?"

"Okay," he responded and we both hung up.

I sat there, thinking about what Toshi said.

These guys deserved punishment. I could try my best to sell out Jam. I could go to the police. I could get help from someone else. Then again, maybe I was the man to take them down. On the other hand, I could have been super high at the moment.

I thought about what had happened. I went in there too hot. Too angry. It had been a long day. My exhaustion was no match for his coked up body. I let that cloud my judgment. I should have put some thought into what I was doing. I had no idea what I was getting into and I was outmatched.

On these mushrooms, I could feel no pain, time had slowed and my thoughts were clearer than they had been for days. I had gone in there and tried to fight the guy. That was my mistake. I wouldn't win a fight with him, so why try.

If a guy was bigger and stronger than me, and my cause was honourable, I had to fight dirty. I wouldn't fight this guy. I would ambush him. I wouldn't try punching him. I would kick him in the nuts. If he got me in one of those holds, I'd bite him as hard as I could. This shit was serious. I would do whatever it takes. I would have to be nasty. The situation called for it. This guy was bragging about people he had killed, it warranted punishment. I am the man that would give him what he deserves. I came to the conclusion that I may have to end the prick's life.

These mushrooms had brought back my confidence. I had no fear and felt stronger than ever. The guy expects me to come walking into his house tomorrow, with my tail between my legs. I will spring on him with a new found conviction. I would end this asshole's reign of terror on the city.

I made my way back to the guy's house and the lights were out this time. I crept around the property with stealth and peered in a few windows. Nobody was home. The Nazi had told me of his yacht and how much time he spent there. I thought that was better. He would never expect me showing up there. It was in the marina for the winter, so I could count on him being in the slip if he was at the yacht. It was worth a shot.

When I made it to the marina I saw him. He was standing on the bow of his yacht smoking a cigar. I ducked behind some barrels. I didn't want him to see me. I watched him as he finished his cigar looking out toward downtown. Once he went back in the cabin I made my way closer.

I had a plan this time. To attack him before he saw me. Try to land a devastating blow before he knew who or what hit him. Then I would use any method of fighting I had in my arsenal, which included biting, hair pulling and whatever else I thought would give me an advantage. I was higher than shit on mushrooms and I was ready to take on an army. Confidence was not going to be an issue, neither was pain. If he landed one of those fancy kicks I would keep going.

I crept up to his boat and crawled my way on board. I climbed up on top of the cabin and positioned myself above the door I had seen him go in. So far things were working surprisingly well. He would have to come out sooner or later. Hopefully sooner, it was cold out.

It wasn't five minutes before I heard the latch on the door. I was standing now, ready to strike. He had no idea I was there when he came sauntering out the door. I jumped down and dropped on him with my knee. He turned when he must have sensed me coming. My knee dropped on top of his head. A good start. He was confused, angry and most likely groggy. He went down to the ground but turned to see me.

"You. You fucking idiot. I'll fucking kill you."

Yup. He was pissed. He came at me throwing a number of punches and quick combos. I kept my hands up and took some glancing blows as he moved closer. When he got in tight enough, I grabbed him by the hair. He squealed as I pulled him towards my other fist. He pulled away and a handful of hair stayed in my fingers. I tossed it aside and tried to keep on the offense. As I neared him, he threw a kick that landed on its mark in my rib cage. Instead of keeling over, the mushrooms dulled any pain. I caught his leg and spun him around, throwing him towards the cabin. I intended to slam him up against the wall but he wound up crashing through a window. Aiming a body being thrown is not a science. I couldn't argue with the results regardless. I jumped in after him. He was bleeding all over his fancy carpet from fresh cuts to his body.

I attempted to step in and land the type of punch that ends fights. He was still quick enough to duck the punch, no matter how injured he was. As he ducked, he grabbed my arm and I got spun around and put in a choke hold before I knew what happened. It was deep but he was bringing his second arm in to lock the hold when his hand went past my face. I didn't hesitate and took a chomp at his hand and caught two fingers. His blood ran from my mouth as I clamped down. The hold eased enough for me to push off. He looked down at the damage on his hands when I grabbed his coffee mug he had on the table and smashed it upside his head. He went down hard. This time he wasn't getting up.

He was out cold. I hoped not for too long, I still needed him for information. I checked his breathing just in case. Luckily I didn't kill him. I decided to tie him to a chair while I had him at a complete disadvantage.

He came to after a minute. I was still tightening the knots. Confused, he was tugging at the duct tape. You could see he couldn't recall what had happened. His blurry vision finally took shape of me, standing over him.

"You cheap fucking cunt." He spit blood and tried to muster out some additional curses and homophobic insults.

He squirmed in the chair, trying to pull free. It rocked back and forth as he got aggressive.

There happened to be a golf bag in the corner of the cabin. I sauntered over and grabbed a nine iron. I walked back to the pile of human sitting in the chair. I spun the club in my hand.

"Do you even golf? These things are brand new, never used. Do you buy stuff for the sake of buying stuff or what?"

"Shut the fuck up. I will fucking kill you." It made him angrier when I talked smack about him.

"Do you so desperately want to appear like a normal Wall Street rich guy, or what is your deal?" I was still checking out the club. The things cost thousands of dollars and he had never swung them.

"I am rich," he tried to say with pride, though he was currently bleeding on himself tied to a chair on his own boat.

"Nah, you are a drug dealer and a murderer. Not some classy playboy you pretend to be. You are a gangster. A common thug." It was amazing to see how angry this made him.

"Fuck you. I am an entrepreneur. I came from nothing, unlike most of the old money white boys running around here. I am better than them."

"You mean the guys you want to fit in with? Just so you know, you will never fit in."

The guy had a serious problem with his identity. I watched him squirm and struggle to break free. I would leave him with his demons. I needed to find my girlfriend.

"You showed me mercy once, and I am willing to do the same. Just tell me where I find him."

"I ain't telling you shit!" he was screaming at me.

"I figured you would say that. You know," I paused to jump onto the coffee table in front of his chair and take my golf stance. I did the golf waggle they do, "I am not very skilled at this game. Sometimes I take some big divots, especially with this backwards lefty club," I lined up the club next to his knee. He began to scream random gibberish. I wasn't going to pay attention until he told me what I wanted to hear.

I was swinging with the wrong hand when I wound up the club. I came down with the club head direct to his knee. He let out a blood curdling scream.

"Damn," I said, "it's going to be hard to do those fancy kicks you do with that knee now. It is one thing to sacrifice your kicking ability for your boss, but I am much better right handed." I turned the club backwards and lined up the back of the club head to his right knee, "Are you willing to sacrifice your ability to walk?"

He was pleading with me now. Begging me not to do it. I had little sympathy for him since he had such an easy way out. I explained this to him, but I think his hatred for me was deep enough that he wanted to see this through. I took a long slow backswing.

"Stop. Stop. Stop!" he was yelling. "I'll tell you what you need to know."

I thought he would try to skimp on details, tell me obvious lies, but he ranted about the guy. He was being truthful.

He was afraid I would bust him up. Mission accomplished. Not that I was bluffing anyway.

"Now let me go. I gotta get to the hospital man."

I sat there thinking for some time. I didn't know how to proceed. If I let this guy go, he would definitely want to kill me. He may not be capable of doing so now, but when he was healthy he would come after me. This could come at any time. I didn't want to be looking over my shoulder the rest of my life. I had to get rid of him. I didn't think I could kill this guy in cold blood. Not while tied up. That is some evil shit. I wasn't that guy.

I decided on a different fate. Thinking of the trophies, the drugs, the cash, and all he had between this yacht and his house, he would never get out of prison. I only needed the police to find it all.

I took his cell phone from his pocket and started dialling.

"What are you doing?" he asked.

"I am sorry, but you are dangerous. I can't trust you not to come after me or my girlfriend. I either call the cops, or I kill you. I take it you would rather take your chances with the police." I pressed talk on the 911 call.

I gave him up, served on a silver platter, as an anonymous tip. He was cursing me out the entire time. Threatening me.

"What makes you think I won't give you up?" He kept yelling.

I asked him what he had on me.

"I no longer have the Red Leaf. It is gone. I wasn't lying about that. I am now clean. I am just a plumber trying to make his way. All you can do is tell them I'm the one that called you in. I'll tell them you tried to kill me. You showed me your trophies as your ritual before you killed me. I escaped after your savage beating," I pointed to my face, "and I will go on to be a hero. I will make the talk show circuit. I will be famous. I may get to meet Oprah. Go ahead tell them about me."

I walked out of the cabin and off the boat. He was still cursing my name.

Chapter 25-8

I was close. Aida had to be there. I had to make it through one last man. I wasn't going to make my previous mistakes though. I thought it through. I surveyed the address that Judo McKickmyface had told me. It was a castle. Right on the edge of central park. A beautiful four story brick mansion. The place had the structure of an old hotel. I walked by it often and had assumed it still was. Obviously, this guy sold a lot more drugs than I did.

People were crawling all over. They appeared to be hired goons. While surveilling the residence I recognized some goombas I had met before. Leonardo came out to talk to the doormen a couple times. I had no way to see what was happening inside the house, or how many guys were in there. It didn't take long before I realized I wasn't going to be able to do this on my own. If I was going to go in to get Aida from this fortress, I would need reinforcements. After some deliberation, I made my way back home.

I went and saw G for the first time since it started. My face must have looked as bad as it felt. The concern he showed when he opened the door even concerned me. I told him the whole story. I don't know what an appropriate reaction should have been, but G's was only one of pure anger for not coming to him sooner. He was mad for not including him since the beginning. He ranted at me for several minutes before I had to cut him off. His concern for me was both valid and adorable, but I needed his help now. I didn't have to say more. It didn't matter how dangerous it would be. He was in.

I told him what I witnessed at the fortress. We were trying to formulate a plan when there was an unexpected knock on the door. I pulled the door open to see the last person I had time for. It was Dubs.

"Not now Dubs, I'm busy," I said as I tried to close the door on him. He stopped me and pushed the door open.

"Jesus, what the fuck happened to your face?"

"Don't worry about it," I replied. "I'm busy though, so if you don't mind," I pointed at the door.

"Look, I came here to talk to you about Aida. She hasn't been returning Daisy's calls. Thanksgiving dinner was last night and we were expecting you two. It's not like you guys to no show. Aida isn't answering her phone and yours has been going straight to voicemail. If you want to ignore me, that's one thing. But Aida is important to Daisy and Daisy is important to me, so I need to know what the fuck is going on."

I didn't know how to respond. So G did. He told him about the whole ordeal, ignoring any of my interjections. G asked if he could help. A stunned Dubs stared at the floor for a minute before responding.

"I'm in. Whatever you need me to do. Let's fuck these guys up." Just like that, we were a three man smashing crew. I was mad at G for bringing Dubs into it, but the extra pair of hands may have been necessary. We went back to the castle and attempted to find consensus on a strategy.

The fucking goombas were everywhere. There was no way we would be able to just walk in and get her. I had an idea. Nobody was a fan of it. Mostly because it was pretty fucking stupid. We kept trying to think of a new strategy, but none of us could settle on anything better.

Fire was our only answer.

We grabbed a can of gasoline from a nearby gas station and strategically placed several puddles around the building when the guards were not paying attention. Then it was time to make it happen. It was five in the afternoon. Between rush hour and foot traffic emergency services would take a couple extra minutes. We designed a couple of molotov cocktails. Gasoline, a dirty rag we stole from the station and some empty glass bottles we took off a homeless man's cart. MacGyvered the shit out of those things. I was now armed with two fireballs.

There were two guards at the front door. G ran up and blindsided the first guy with a right hook that put him on his ass. The second guard came at him and G took off in full sprint. He rounded the corner and passed right by Dubs. That guard didn't recognize the pudgy bastard, and his legs buckled when he took a punch to the nose while in full sprint. Had there been no punch to the face it would have been one of the sweetest dance moves ever. Apparently you look smooth when you lose consciousness and can't control your muscles at full speed. Unfortunately, his sweet move landed him on the pavement where Dubs dragged him into the nearby bushes. Dubs was laughing his ass off.

"You see how I folded him in half? You can't punch a man harder," he said with pride.

"I told you this change would come in handy." G said as they both opened their hands to show the roll of quarters they were holding. Punching a man with those in your hand was like hitting them with a brick. The natural give your fist has is gone. They may as well have used brass knuckles.

It wasn't a bad idea, so I took a roll of quarters off of G.

With the front door guards out of the way, I took one Molotov cocktail, lit the fuse, and ran towards the castle. I threw it at the exterior of the building, lighting the gas we had poured. The fire surrounded the structure. Then I ran around to the front door. This was it. I prayed it would work, despite its stupidity. I lit the second fireball. I was about to kick in the front door when I remembered destroying my body going through the roof access door running away from goons before. That had hurt. This time I tried the door. Unlocked. Way easier. Inside the house it still looked like an old hotel. I stepped in to see a large foyer in front of some stairs. I tossed in the second fireball into the middle of the room. Then we waited.

People piled out of every exit in a hurry. There were guys coming down the fire escapes, out the side doors and out the windows. A chair flew through one window on the first floor and this mammoth of a man tried to climb out. He struggled and tipped over, flipping out the window. He was now cut up and bleeding from the broken glass. I was almost impressed by his ability to keep his cool and not panic.

There was a fair amount of smoke, but the place did not look like it would go up that fast. It was mostly stone. We decided it was better to move quickly though. Dubs, G and I headed for the front door and ran around the scorching hot bonfire I had created in the foyer. Inside, it was spreading fast enough to grab onto the walls and climb curtains. Seeing this, I got concerned it could happen faster than I thought. The bonfire in the middle of the house was burning a round hole in the ceiling above it. I was not keen on burning my girlfriend alive while trying to rescue her. We had to find her fast.

We made it up the stairs with only a few people remaining. They mostly ignored us running in the opposite direction. Turns out hired goons are worthless when there is a fire. Never trust your life to a man you pay to be brave. I am certain most are cowards. Otherwise they would have done something with their life on their own. At least the plan was working.

The building turned out to actually be an old hotel. They hadn't bothered to remove their fire prevention system. It wasn't doing them a lot of good at the moment. Walking up the stairs I discovered a box on the wall at the landing. It was an axe encased, the glass saying 'Break in Case of Emergency'. I couldn't think of any better time to do this.

I put my elbow through the pane of glass and grabbed the large red handle. I thought it could come in handy. I continued up the stairs. Dubs took the second floor and G took the third. Everyone was to sweep the place and find her. Then we would clear out before the fire got too dangerous. I intentionally chose the top floor, it being the most dangerous and most likely place for me to find Aida according to Judo.

I made my way around the floor which had a theme of medieval decorations. There were statues, armor, shields and shit decorating the halls. I carefully made my way, opening each door. I went from one room to another clearing the floor. Nobody had stayed behind. Drugs filled one room and it looked like they controlled the distribution from there. The room was left surprisingly unattended. His hired help was useless. A gym was in the next room, covered in mirrors. Another room housed a huge aquarium filled with what I believed to be piranhas. This guy was such an ass. Every door I opened made me want to beat the shit out of him worse. Smoke was filling the hallway. I got to the end of the hall and turned the corner to see four guys still in the building guarding a large double door. I was heading in the right direction. It was the four turtles. I put my axe down. It wouldn't help me in a situation with four people. It would only slow the process and the fire was becoming an issue.

No one said a word as I placed the axe on the floor. Two of them came at me. Leonardo and Raphael. They ran down the hallway towards me. The two others were sure to follow so I needed to make the window of opportunity count. I wanted to take out the biggest guy first. It makes the others nervous. Luckily, Leonardo was the biggest and also the fearless leader, so he was the first to make it to me. One punch was all it took. The roll of quarters broke in my hand and they fell to the ground as I followed through on his chin. His jaw broke. In several places. He should have taken his time instead of walking right into it. Raphael was still coming at me. The other two that had begun moving towards me slowed as they watched Leo twitch his leg on the ground. Raph was furious and threw a combination of punches. I had to stick to blocking my face. I no longer had my roll of knockout quarters so I was tentative. However, I had to end it quick before the other two came back to their senses. I was blocking the barrage of punches as Raphael got closer and closer to me. He was in so tight I turned on him and fed an elbow to his chin. It stopped him dead in his tracks. He fell to the ground and I proceeded to give him two quick kicks to the ribs, breaking at least one. The next part of my plan required those broken bones. The two incapacitated bodies would need tending to.

The other two guys were standing there, unsure what to do next. I made the decision for them.

"If you guys want to stay alive and save your friends," I pointed to the two on the ground, Leo not moving and Raphael groaning in pain, "you should leave now and help them out. They won't get out of this building on their own with their injuries. You are going to have to help them. This is your only chance. You don't owe that douche." I pointed to the door behind them. "I'll take care of him."

They looked at each other and then nodded in agreement to me. I back peddled and picked up my axe. They helped their buddies to their feet for evacuation and hobbled by me. I held my weapon at the ready in case they changed their minds.

Once they were by, I made my way to the door they had been guarding. The locked door was nothing an axe couldn't handle. I put it through the door next to the knob. I knew the situation was serious, so I didn't perform my 'Here's Johnny!' yell that crossed my mind. Screaming "It's-a Me!" for some reason seemed appropriate, but I withheld that one too. I reached in the hole and unlocked the door.

I entered the master bedroom. Through the smoke I saw my girl, my princess. My heart skipped a beat while relief washed over me to see her face. The relief was short lived. The douchebag was tying her to a chair in the corner of the room. When she looked my way and recognized I was there, she screamed for me. My heart raced and I wanted to run to her, but he stood up from behind the chair he was affixing my girlfriend to. Next to him was a dog. A pit bull. I fucking knew it.

"Nice of you to join us. I had a feeling this was your doing. So you know, I plan on leaving your girlfriend in this chair. That way, once I have beaten you to a pulp, you can lie on my floor and burn to death. You can still stare her straight in the eyes and admit to her that this was your fault."

"You don't have to do this, you can let her go. She has nothing to do with this," I pleaded.

"How fucking cliché. She has everything to do with this. You have been running around, trying to destroy my whole network. You are the reason my man got arrested a few hours ago aren't you? You think you are tough? I want you to hurt, to feel pain. I'll make you feel it. Having her here to watch will make it even better."

He paused and looked down at his dog, "Get'em Boom Boom."

The dog ran right at me. These breeds are ferocious bastards, but I wasn't too concerned about a tiny dog. I did feel bad I had to hurt it. The animal didn't understand that his owner was such an asshole. At this point though, it was me or the mutt and I was going to have to do it. I had to stop it with simple timing. As he approached I jumped into the air and came down just in time to place my foot on top of his mouth. It prevented any chance for him to latch on to me. I probably broke its jaw. Took away any fight it had in it, so it went whimpering into the corner.

The ginger was pissed. He no doubt had feelings for that dog. For some unknown reason he had a tool belt lying on the nightstand next to him. He must have been working on a project earlier or he used it for intimidation tactics. Either way he picked the hammer out of the belt and wound up as if he was going to hit Aida with it. She winced and tried her best to pull away, but she was stuck to that damn chair. I let out a loud blood curdling scream to get his attention.

"Come on man, your beef is with me. If you take her out, it won't be my fault with the fire and trying to rescue her. Wouldn't that be satisfying? Come over this way, fight me like a man," I put the axe down on the floor. "Come on you fucking douche. You afraid of me?" I pleaded with him, trying to antagonize him.

He walked towards me. As he got closer he wound up and threw the hammer. I wasn't expecting that. I thought he would want to hold on to the weapon, so I didn't exactly react. Luckily, the hammer went flying over top my head. That could have fucking hurt.

I was still counting my lucky stars from the missed hammer when he stepped into me and punched me right in the guts. I keeled over in agony. Turns out he was big but still agile enough to throw a punch. I think I wheezed.

I had one knee on the floor and was trying to stand back up when he dropped another punch onto my chin. It was still tender from the beating I had taken the day before. The mushrooms had worn off at this point, so it hurt like a motherfucker. Before he could continue his onslaught, I rolled backwards on the ground to get away. I had to get my feet underneath me and regain composure. I took my time getting up and thought about my next move.

I needed to slow the guy down. I had to target a weak spot, but this guy was one giant muscle. I would have to go for joints. His knees. I thought I could take a page out of the previous dick's book and try a kick. It may not have been the best time to be trying new moves. He was coming at me quick though, and I had to find a way to slow him down. He came in close and I kicked as hard as I could at his right knee. It was successful in the fact that it landed. I don't know what hurt more though, his knee or my foot. Now we both hobbled after each other. I tried to keep my distance. I backpedalled and let him be the aggressor. I snuck in a few punches when he came within range. When he finally managed to get in tight, we both exchanged blows. It was like he grew tired of it and decided to change it up. He grabbed on to me, picked me up, and threw me. It might have been a distance record. I would have looked like a rag doll. You wouldn't think it would hurt that much, but I might as well have fallen from the roof of the building. I coughed and sputtered as he came walking toward me. I needed to recover. I got up and continued to back away to pull myself together.

It had become a mess of a fight. I needed to improve to end this quicker. The fire was engulfing the building and the smoke buildup was causing us both to cough and hack. Meanwhile we were trying to engage in physical combat.

He came at me hard. He was at a full sprint and jumped in the air for a superman punch. I was quick enough to duck under. When he passed me I had a free moment to throw some right hooks into his rib cage and midsection. I pushed him across the room to try keep behind him. He succeeded in turning himself around but the punches I landed were hard enough that I saw him spit blood. Something had ruptured. Now I was getting somewhere.

He stood at the other side of the room. I should have made a move at him while I had him hurt. We were both exhausted and bloodied. Many of my previous wounds had opened up, and there were now fresh ones leaking down my cheeks. I had landed at least a few damaging blows on him, which was causing his nose to flow.

The room was full of smoke. It was seeping through the floorboards in the middle of the room. We were above the foyer where the fire had started. I could feel the floor getting warmer through my shoes.

I was standing between him and Aida and the axe was lying on the floor next to me. I picked it back up. I thought I could maybe let Aida out of the chair if I could keep him back. She would at least get to escape the building while we finished this. I could also try chopping the fucking guy's head clean off at the same time. He didn't give me the chance to get to Aida. He came running at me. With an axe in my hand, he still showed no restraint. He threw a punch that looked like he tried to kill me with it. I avoided it and his follow through kept his momentum going another three steps past me. We both stood at the ready, jockeying for position, waiting for the right moment. I maneuvered around him to get back between him and Aida. It backed him up to the floor where smoke was coming through. His eyes were watering and I could see him struggling with the smoke. I wound up and swung the axe with full force. He jumped back and my axe landed in front of him and stuck in the floor.

I pulled the axe loose and tried to keep him back. He attempted to get closer and closer to me, so I swung the axe again, forcing him to jump back again. I was quick to pull the axe out of the floor before he came at me while it was stuck. We played this game several times. He continued to try get at me, and I continued to hold him back with a swing of the axe.

"What do you think you are doing?" He asked. "Put the axe down. It serves you no purpose. You will just keep us here until we all die. Using your words, fight me like a man."

The smoke was venting into the room through the floor and worse through the holes created by the axe. Some loud creaks, moans and groans came from below us. I saw it in his eyes when he realized what was happening. Before he had a chance to move I swung the axe one more time.

The floor was weak and he was a heavy man. He jumped forward as my axe came down. He landed just shy of the damage and the hardwood crumbled under his weight. The axe fell through and into the fiery abyss. He was lucky to catch himself on the remaining floor where a beam was still holding together. He had both elbows up and was dangling his feet below.

He was kicking his feet and trying his best to pull himself up. Without leverage for his legs below, he dangled there unable to lift up his own weight. He stared at me as I walked over and bent down so I could stare him right in the eyes. I grabbed his two arms and simply said, "Fuck you," and flung him into the fiery four storey hell hole below.

I ran over to my tied up girlfriend and freed her from the rope. She threw her arms around me. Unfortunately, I had to tell her we didn't have time for that kind of shit. I was ecstatic to have her in my arms, but with the giant hole in the middle of the room, the smoke had now become unbearable. We needed a way out fast. We checked outside the window, no fire escape. It was outside the room next to us. The fire trucks were just arriving. We didn't have time to wait for a ladder with the lack of oxygen about to choke us out. I also preferred not to explain what we were doing in the drug dealer's burning building in the first place. Contemplating a move towards the doorway, the floor in front of us gave way, causing flames to erupt into the room. I was not too keen on walking around the pit or jumping over. I was unsure of the integrity of the whole building at this point.

As I surveyed the room, I saw the dog. He was still cowering in the corner, whimpering and afraid. I couldn't allow him to stay in there so I ran over and picked him up. He was too terrified of the fire to be scared or fight with the man who hurt him.

With a dog cradled in my arms and a girl clasping to my shirt sleeve I checked out the only other window in the room. It was a narrow alleyway. Maybe five feet across. There was a window about four feet lower than the one we were currently looking out of. It was not going to be the safest maneuver in the world, but it happened to be our only hope. I got Aida to hold the dog and lie down on the floor. We were both coughing and my eyes were burning. We did not have much time. I ran to check out front and still saw no sign of an imminent rescue. I grabbed the chair Aida had previously been affixed to and swung it through the front window. The glass rained down on the people below. I could hear screams from the street as people were no doubt gathered to watch the flames engulf the building. This sucked the fumes and heat out the window and I damn near choked and blacked out.

It did create some brief visibility in the room as things vented. Aida began screaming for me. I made my way over to her and told her what we were going to have to do.

"Aida, the firemen are not going to make it in time to help us. We are going to have to jump."

"Are you fucking insane? It's four fucking stories."

"Not to the ground. I think we can make the jump into that building across the way. See the window right there? Take a big jump and make it through. I'll go first and I will clear the glass and be ready to catch you when you go. We have to do it babe. It's our only chance."

"I don't think I can do this." She was afraid. Rightly so. It was lunacy. It also happened to be our only choice.

"I know it's scary, but I will not let you fall, alright? Look at me. I will not let you fall," I said firmly.

"I love you," she told me, sounding defeated.

"Save that shit for when we are safe on the ground, okay?" I responded as reassuringly as I could.

I used the chair again. This time I chucked it through the glass. The chair shattered to splinters in the alley below. It was a long way down. I surveyed the scene and lined up the jump across the alley. It did not look easy. There was a suitcase on the floor next to us that I figured I could put to use. It was the perfect size and heavy enough to bust the window in the adjacent building. This would at least prevent my body from having to do it. I picked it up on my shoulder and took two steps as I shot put it right on target. It was a perfect toss that went directly through the window. It left some jagged edges, but this was going to have to get done. I picked up the dog and tucked him under my arm like a football. I thought about what was happening. There was a four story chasm between me and a fiery death. I was going to make the jump. I stared Aida right in the eyes and psyched myself up to start my run.

"As soon as I jump, get ready to go and I'll be waiting for you." She nodded in agreement, terrified. I felt sick for what had I gotten this poor girl into.

I took my three step approach, reached the opening and jumped with everything I had. I tucked myself into as small of a ball as I could to avoid shredding myself on broken glass. I headed right for the opening and was going to make the straight shot which was comforting. I did not want to have to drop the dog if I needed to grab the ledge. My arms and legs got destroyed by the remaining glass as I passed through. I was bleeding from my extremities instead of just my face. I put the dog on the ground and picked up a nearby umbrella. I used it to clear out the remaining shards from the windowsill so Aida had a better chance of doing it unharmed. I could see her quivering from above, sticking her head out for fresh air. The smoke was billowing out. There couldn't have been much oxygen left in there.

"I need you to jump. I will catch you."

I put one leg outside and kept one in, straddling to reach out if necessary. I could hear her coughing over the roaring fire.

"Come on baby. Do it. Do it now." I was panicking. If she hesitated any longer she could succumb to the smoke. I wouldn't have been able to get back in there to help her.

She emerged from the smoke, running towards the jump. Diving through head first, her aim and velocity looked good. She was going to make it. I stuck my arms out to grab her, but it was more her tackling me. We fell into the building. She lay on top of me, still coughing and sputtering. We remained there for what felt like an eternity. It was probably only a minute. She finally leaned up after her coughing fit only to start slapping me furiously. She was crying, screaming at me, while she attacked me relentlessly.

"I'm sorry, I am so sorry," I was repeating over and over.

When she finally finished slapping me, we fell into an embrace and I never wanted to let her go. I asked in her ear if I could take her home. She only nodded in her exhaustion. As we were standing up to leave, she froze.

"Look," she said, pointing at the suitcase I had thrown through the windows. Bulging at the seams, the zipper had come undone and cash was spilling out. Banded cash. I didn't care to stare at it any longer or wonder how much was in there.

We picked it up and wheeled it out. Lucky for us nobody had been home in the apartment we crashed through. We took one of the bundles of cash and left it on the table. Ten grand should cover the damaged window.

There was a mess of fire trucks, police cruisers and ambulances arriving, filling the street. We made our way down from the adjacent building, rolling the suitcase and carrying an injured dog. Firemen surrounded us. They brought us away because they evacuated that building too. They wanted me to get medical attention. I told them my cuts and bruises were an unrelated incident. At the first distraction, Aida and I faded into the crowd and fled the scene.

Baillargeon

Chapter 26

People may wonder what it feels like to kill a man in cold blood. You would think I may feel bad, guilty or have nightmares of some sort. The truth of the matter is, it doesn't faze me for a second. Honestly, I don't have any regret for what I did to him. He made his choice. He tried to hurt me and he hurt my girl. He paid for it with his life.

We met up with G and Dubs after getting out of the building. Nobody had any issues. They had run in and out after clearing their floors. I had Aida and we were going home. We didn't have time to chat. I had to take care of my girl. For the time being we went our separate ways.

The cops eventually blamed the fire on a rival gang. I wasn't the only one he was picking fights with. On the news they said there was only one casualty in the fire, a known drug dealer and suspected murderer. Probably why they didn't investigate too much. I cleaned up what the police couldn't.

- - - - - - -

G is still off on his wacky adventures, trying to make it on his own. I think he is coming to terms with the fact that he can't cut it without his big bro around. When I'm missing, it is just not fun. I give him work from time to time at my place and I hope he soon decides to settle down and work for me full time. He is a good kid and when he learns to become responsible on his own, he is going to be happier for it. I look forward to the day I get to tell my mom he has met a nice girl.

I owed Dubs for his help, so I bought him a beer once. I am still annoyed I have to see him so often though, even after I quit my job. He still dates Daisy. He makes her happy so he can't be all bad. Maybe I should start to cut him some slack. He did come through for me when I needed him.

As for me, I am out of the drug world. I made enough cash to start my own successful business. I have completely abandoned the plumbing trade and I run a go-kart track and party place. Kids are more my style and they are paying me a fortune. Plus, they deal in cash. Makes it easy for me to pad the books with a suitcase full of it. I'll have this place paid off in no time.

I took a bigger role in Big Brothers. I host events at my party place on the cheap for them. There are kids out there needing some positive influences in their lives. I finally think I am one of them now. It might be time for me to have some of my own.

It took a long time for me to recover with Aida. She was understandably upset. We both took some serious time off work to decompress. We spent days talking about the whole ordeal. Luckily, they did not treat her too bad. The guy thought I was going to come through and get him what he wanted and it would be over. He didn't want to make an enemy of me by mistreating her. He misread that situation.

She told me she spent the majority of her time locked in the bedroom watching television under guard. I was so thankful to hear she went unhurt. For one thing, I don't want any harm to come to her ever. More selfishly, I don't think she could have ever forgiven me if something terrible had happened. I don't think I could have forgiven myself. I couldn't have handled losing her forever.

One of the stipulations of her sticking by my side was obvious. I was out of the drug business and would refrain from doing anything illegal. Except of course for the money laundering. We had to do deal with that. The money had nothing to do with her staying, but it definitely didn't hurt.

The first couple weeks afterward were rocky. She had me under her thumb. Life eventually settled back into its old routines. With time, I was able to win her over again. Our relationship was going so well that I convinced my mother to come back home for Christmas to meet Aida. It upset me it had taken this long already. They hit it off. My mom wouldn't stop commenting on how beautiful she was and hinting at me to not let this one go. I took her advice and didn't waste any time. I proposed a few weeks later.

By February we finally got to take that trip to Hawaii. My mom and her husband, G and his then girlfriend and Dubs and Daisy made it down. They witnessed as Aida and I got married on the beach in a small but beautiful ceremony. I never thought it would happen to me. My peach had now become my wife. We moved out into the suburbs and we also have a rescue dog, Boom Boom, who turned out to be a loving pet.

I learned a lot about life, love and myself. It turns out I might not be the smartest, toughest person around. I was lucky enough to learn this lesson and come out of it okay. Better than okay. I have the girl, and enough cash to spoil her and keep us comfortable. My life is super. I couldn't be happier.

So fuck you Pauline.

Baillargeon